P9-CJC-791

RUBY GOLDBERG'S
Bright Idea

RUBY GOLDBERG'S

Bright Idea

Anna Humphrey

Illustrated by
Vanessa Brantley Newton

WITHDRAWN

Simon & Schuster Books for Young Readers
New York   London   Toronto   Sydney   New Delhi

SIMON & SCHUSTER BOOKS FOR YOUNG READERS
An imprint of Simon & Schuster Children's Publishing Division
1230 Avenue of the Americas, New York, New York 10020

This book is a work of fiction. Any references to historical events, real people, or real places are used fictitiously. Other names, characters, places, and events are products of the author's imagination, and any resemblance to actual events or places or persons, living or dead, is entirely coincidental.
Text copyright © 2014 by Anna Humphrey and Simon & Schuster, Inc.
Illustrations copyright © 2014 by Vanessa Brantley Newton
All rights reserved, including the right of reproduction in whole or in part in any form.
SIMON & SCHUSTER BOOKS FOR YOUNG READERS is a trademark of Simon & Schuster, Inc.

For information about special discounts for bulk purchases, please contact Simon & Schuster Special Sales at 1-866-506-1949 or business@simonandschuster.com.
The Simon & Schuster Speakers Bureau can bring authors to your live event. For more information or to book an event, contact the Simon & Schuster Speakers Bureau at 1-866-248-3049 or visit our website at www.simonspeakers.com.
Book design by Chloë Foglia
The text for this book is set in Bembo.
The illustrations for this book are rendered in a combination of traditional and digital media.
Manufactured in the United States of America
1213 FFG
2 4 6 8 10 9 7 5 3 1
Library of Congress Cataloging-in-Publication Data
Humphrey, Anna.
Ruby Goldberg's bright idea / Anna Humphrey ; illustrations, Vanessa Brantley Newton.—First edition.
pages cm
Summary: Ruby is determined to win the gold with her fifth-grade science fair project, a Rube Goldberg machine to help her grandfather, but the real prize turns out to be something completely unexpected.
ISBN 978-1-4424-8027-8 (hardcover)
ISBN 978-1-4424-8031-5 (eBook)
[1. Science projects—Fiction. 2. Inventions—Fiction. 3. Interpersonal relations—Fiction. 4. Grandfathers—Fiction. 5. Goldberg, Rube, 1883–1970—Fiction. 6. Science fairs—Fiction.] I. Brantley Newton, Vanessa, illustrator. II. Title.
PZ7.H8935Rub 2014
[Fic]—dc23
2013002034

FIRST
F
EDITION

For my dad, who always finds a way to build it—
whatever it may be
—A. H.

To my miracle girl who loves to read, Zoe
—V. B. N.

Acknowledgments

Big thank yous to Julia Maguire and the editorial team at Simon & Schuster Books for Young Readers for dreaming up Ruby and inviting me to write her story, and to Rebecca Friedman of Hill Nadell Literary Agency, who never stops believing.

I also owe more than I can say to Heather MacLeod, who took such good care of my kids while I wrote all summer, and to my dad, who helped me to "build" Ruby's machine on paper. Lastly, a heartfelt thank you to Gwyn for teaching me about dogs (and for being my mom's faithful sidekick for nearly thirteen years). You were a good boy.

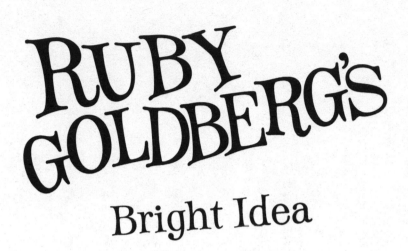

Bright Idea

*"Tomorrow is just another day to create something
I hope will be worthwhile."*

—Rube Goldberg

Chapter 1

Some people don't know how to mind their own business. Dominic Robinson is *definitely* one of them.

It started on Friday afternoon at shared reading time. Every kid in Ms. Slate's fifth-grade class was supposed to be taking turns reading from *Sadako and the Thousand Paper Cranes* while everyone else was supposed to be listening and following along with their finger.

And listening was *exactly* what I was doing—minus the finger part. Because my fingers were busy building something, which is a far better use of fingers, if you ask me.

"Why do you think the author included the spider in chapter one?" Ms. Slate asked the class. "Any ideas?"

"Because it's lucky?" Supeng ventured.

"That's right," Ms. Slate said. "In Japanese culture spiders are considered lucky."

"Or maybe because it might rain?" Eleni suggested. "My yaya says it rains when you see a spider."

I knew a lot about spiders from the Amazing Arachnids exhibit at the Museum of Science in Boston, where my grandpa takes me every month. I was pretty sure the rain thing was only if you *stepped* on the spider . . . and even then it was only a superstition—*not* a scientific fact. Normally I would have set the record straight, but I was a little preoccupied. In a minute we'd be turning the page to chapter two, and my invention wasn't ready yet.

My best friend, Penny, waved from across the room to get my attention. *What are you doing?* she signed. Penny isn't deaf, but her cousin is, so she goes to sign language class on Tuesdays after school to learn how to communicate with him. As an added bonus, it comes in handy when your teacher sits you and your best friend on opposite ends of the room so you'll stop talking.

Making, I signed back, since I didn't know the American Sign Language sign for "inventing." I tilted my book up to show her the clothespin on a string I'd attached to it, then held up my mini battery-powered pocket fan.

C-A-R-E-F-U-L, she finger-spelled back. Then she started twirling a strand of her shiny black hair around one finger, which is always what she does when she's worried. I nodded. Penny was right. Caution was a must. The day before, during silent reading, I'd shared a really cool fact with the class. It was about the Hangzhou Bay Bridge in China, which is twenty-two miles long and crosses an entire ocean! You'd think everyone would have thanked me for the interesting and educational information, right?

Ms. Slate didn't . . . and because it wasn't the first (or second or third) time I'd shared a fact when we were supposed to be reading silently, and because then everyone got distracted from their books and started talking, she kept the whole class in for part of recess.

Plus there was the time the week before when I'd accidentally broken the candy jar on her desk because I'd wanted to be first in line for the Friday treat, and then *nobody* got to have a Hershey's Kiss.

"You know, Ruby . . . not everything has to be a contest of who's first," Ally had said, sighing as she'd packed away her notebooks that day. "Now you ruined the greatest part of the week for everyone."

"Yeah . . . ," Colin had agreed. "Just like you ruined the honey field trip last year because you were showing off."

Okay—that hadn't been exactly my fault. When we'd visited a real working beehive last fall, the bee tender had gone on and on about how bees pollinate flowers (which everyone already knew). She hadn't even mentioned the really interesting part—how bees communicate by dancing. So I'd helped her out with a short demonstration. Not that anyone had appreciated it.

"You owe us honey *and* chocolate now," Colin had added. Then he'd stormed off behind Ally.

I didn't mean to ruin things, of course. But didn't everyone want to be first in line? And didn't people want to know interesting things? I knew I definitely did!

All the same, Penny was right to warn me about my invention. I couldn't afford to get in trouble again, or even *she* might get mad at me—not that she did that very often. As best friends went, Penny was amazingly patient, which was a good thing, because sometimes dealing with me took a lot of patience.

"Colin, would you start us off on chapter two?" Ms. Slate asked. The rustling of paper filled the air as everyone turned the page and Colin began. This was it. Ready or not, it was time to test the Ruby Goldberg Page-o-Matic (patent pending).

I could picture the infomercial already: *Why strain yourself turning hundreds of pages? Get the Page-o-Matic today! With one easy motion you can pull the string attached to the clothespin, which opens to release the page and tilts the ruler, which hits the button that turns on the fan that blows the page over for you!*

Or at least in theory it did—unless the clothespin wasn't attached quite right. In which case it might come sproinging off the book and hit someone in the head.

"Ouch!" Brianne glared at me from across the aisle and rubbed her ear. "Ruby!" she said under her breath.

"Sorry," I whispered. Luckily, Colin was having trouble

pronouncing a Japanese word from the book, and Ms. Slate was so busy helping him that she hadn't noticed the attack of the flying clothespin.

I pulled on the string to reel the clothespin back to my desk. Then I reattached the clothespin, firmly, to the book.

"Pssst. Ruby!" Dominic Robinson—a.k.a. the nosiest kid I know—leaned across the aisle on my other side. His thick brown hair fell into his eyes, like it always does, and he blinked out from underneath it. I couldn't quite put my finger on it, but there was something about him that always reminded me of a turtle. "Try propping this under the fan." He held out a pencil case with cartoon dogs on it. "It'll give you a better angle."

Now, don't get me wrong. Even though he's a first-class snoop, I won't deny that Dominic Robinson is good at many things . . . multiplying with decimal places, acing every science test, sharpening his pencils to perfect points . . . but whispering in class is *not* one of them. He was talking WAY too loudly. Plus, he was looking right at me. Even the most amateur whisperer knows that the way to avoid getting caught is to look straight ahead!

"At shared reading time we show respect to our classmates by listening," Ms. Slate reminded the whole room, but she was looking right at us when she said it. Dominic was still holding out the pencil case to me. I grabbed it and shoved it under my desk before we could get in any more trouble.

As Colin kept reading, I went back to work, looping the

string on the clothespin more tightly so that I could control the tension better.

"Ally, would you read next?" Ms. Slate asked.

As everyone turned the page, I pulled carefully on my string. The clothespin opened. The page was released. The ruler tipped, hitting the button on the fan, which whirred to life, only—ACK! Dominic had been right. The angle of the fan was wrong. Instead of blowing page nine over, the fan rustled page eight uselessly. I didn't have much time. Without thinking, I grabbed Dominic's pencil case and propped it underneath. Only, I shoved just a little too hard, and all of a sudden—*CRASH!*

The entire Ruby Goldberg Page-o-Matic smashed to the floor, along with my book and Dominic's pencil case, which spewed markers everywhere. The pocket fan leapt and vibrated in crazy circles like some kind of deranged beetle, then smacked loudly into the leg of Dominic's desk and went dead.

"Ruby!" Ms. Slate said, walking down the aisle. "What, may I ask, are you doing now?"

"Turning the page," I answered. It was the honest truth. I bent over and picked up the string, ruler, and clothespin, then started to collect the spilled markers.

Ms. Slate sighed. "Next time see if you can turn the page without disrupting the entire class." A bunch of kids at the front laughed. "There's a time and place for experimenting and making inventions," she went on, eyeing the collection of stuff on my desk, "and it isn't during shared reading time . . . or math . . . or language arts . . . or community circle. We've talked about this before."

"I know," I said, tilting my head to one side and making my best, most angelic apology face. It wasn't even that hard to do, because I *was* sorry. I didn't mean to be disruptive. It was just that ideas had a way of rushing into my brain and filling it up so full that there was barely room left to focus on anything else.

"Books away," Ms. Slate said, letting the subject drop. "We'll keep reading on Monday. Before the bell rings, we need to talk about the science fair, anyway."

Now she had my full attention. Along with Nature Week— when we got to take walks and study trees and bugs—the science fair was my favorite thing of the year. Two years ago, I'd taken the bronze medal for making a pinhole camera . . . and last year I'd won silver for my digital clock that ran on lemon juice.

"Here." Dominic picked my pocket fan up off the floor and set it on the edge of my desk. It immediately rolled off again. "Oh. Sorry," he said.

But even though bronze and silver were good, they *weren't* gold! Dominic had won first prize the past two years—in third grade with a project where he'd taken apart and studied the inside of a digital camera, and then last year with a full-size grandfather clock that had run on the energy from potatoes. Both clear rip-offs of my ideas! Not that the judges had seemed to notice or care.

Dominic bent down, picked the pocket fan up again, and handed it to me this time. "Thanks," I said coldly. After all, if he'd been minding his own business and reading *Sadako*, he wouldn't have noticed me building the Page-o-Matic, or passed me his stupid pencil case. Then I wouldn't have dropped my stuff and gotten in trouble in the first place. And, more important, if it hadn't been for his copycat photography project and potato clock, *I* would have won the gold medal—or at least the silver—two years running.

Sure, Dominic appeared harmless enough with his blinky eyes, "helpful" suggestions, and cartoon doggy pencil case, but only I knew the truth. Underneath those overgrown bangs lurked a cunning, spying, ruthless science project-stealer who would stop at nothing to win.

Well, not this year, I thought as I took a science fair sign-up sheet off the top of the pile and passed the others back. This year Ruby Goldberg was going for gold, and nobody—especially not Dominic Robinson—was going to stop me.

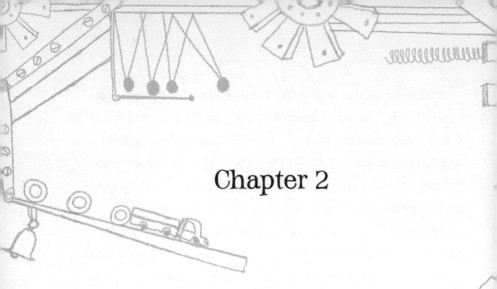

Chapter 2

On Friday afternoons most kids switch the channel in their brains the second the bell rings. They turn off thoughts of school and homework to focus on skateboarding, swimming, video games, and other weekend stuff. Penny was no exception. As we walked to my grandpa's house that afternoon, she talked nonstop about the dance practice she had coming up on Saturday, and how her mom was sewing individual sequins onto some kind of Chinese peacock outfit for her final recital.

But then there are other kids, like me, who—Friday or not Friday—can't seem to stop thinking about school stuff—or, okay, in my case, science fair stuff.

"I have to practice my hand like this for the peacock

dance," Penny was saying, making a beak kind of shape with her fingers. "It's way harder than it looks."

"Mmm-hmmmm," I answered thoughtfully. "Peacocks," I whispered under my breath. Maybe for my science project I could visit the zoo and investigate why peacocks spread their feathers to attract a mate. . . .

It wasn't that I didn't care about Penny's dance thing, but with the science fair right around the corner and Dominic out to get me, I didn't exactly have time to waste. I felt a tickle on my leg and reached down to brush off an ant—which made my mind race off in another direction. Ants! I could keep an ant farm and study their tunneling habits. Only, what would my hypothesis be? "Ants like to dig?" Everybody knows that.

"Miss Leung says the Chinese peacock dance is the most important folk dance in the Dai culture, so we need to do it just right, out of respect." Penny was still talking. "I'm kind of worried. Do you think I'll do a good enough job? I mean, I've been practicing hard, but . . ."

I pressed the button on the crosswalk, and the lights started flashing. We waited for the traffic to stop, and then crossed carefully. Then again, I thought, peacocks were pretty, and ants were interesting, but animals weren't exactly my area of expertise. Except for my grandpa's dog, Tomato, I'd never even had a pet in my family. I was more into the mechanics of things—like how, exactly, when I pressed the crosswalk button, did the energy flow up to the sign and make it start to flash?

"Ruby?" Penny said. "Earth to Ruby . . ."

"Uh-huh," I answered.

"Are you even listening to me?"

"Of course I am!" I said. I'd caught the basics. "Your peacock costume is going to look great. Your mom's a great sewer. Don't worry."

Penny just kind of sighed, shook her head, and smiled. "You're thinking about the science fair, aren't you?" she said. "I can tell."

"Maybe a little," I admitted. I pulled a flower off a bush as we passed and studied its stamen. Maybe I could do something about plants? But Supeng had done an experiment with bean sprouts the year before where she'd played them classical music to see if they would grow faster, and the results hadn't been very conclusive. "I need to come up with something really good," I explained. "There's no way I'm letting Dominic win gold—especially not after he stole my last two ideas."

Penny tilted her head to one side, giving me her most patient look. It wasn't the first time we'd had this conversation. "You know we still don't have any proof of that," she said.

"Proof!" I spat back. "*I* did a photography project. *He* did a photography project. *I* made a lemon clock. *He* made a potato clock. What more proof do you need?"

"I know. I know," Penny said, trying to calm me down. "It's just . . . maybe he didn't mean to copy you. There are only so many ideas for science projects out there."

"There are a million ideas for science projects!" I said, looking around wildly. A gnarled old tree caught my eye. "You could study the life cycle of tree fungus! Or figure out why leaves change color in the fall!"

"Why *do* they turn red and brown in the fall?" Penny asked, looking up. It was early October, but it had been so warm that we were wearing T-shirts, and most of the leaves were still on the trees. "That would make a great project."

I looked at her like she was crazy. "It's because they stop making chlorophyll when it gets cold," I explained. "When the green fades, the other colors in the leaves start to show." There was a whole chapter about it in the tree book I'd had since third grade. It was interesting, but not really fifth-grade-gold-medal-science-project material.

"Anyway . . . ," I said, going back to the more important topic we were discussing. "Dominic just has no creativity— and he's *so* snoopy. Did you see him staring at my invention and then handing me that pencil case, practically right in front of Ms. Slate's nose? Why couldn't he just mind his own business . . . or make his own invention if he was that interested?"

As we approached my grandpa's house, we could see that his neighbor, Mr. Petrecelli, was out on his porch trying to hunt down a fly with a rolled up newspaper.

"Hi, Mr. Petrecelli," Penny called out, although I wasn't sure why she bothered. The old man just kind of grunted in response, which was all he ever did. Well, that and yell if we stepped so much as one foot on his precious lawn.

"Ha!" he exclaimed, totally ignoring us and swinging his newspaper down hard against the railing. When he saw that he'd successfully squashed the fly, he looked almost happy, but only for a second. Then he tossed the newspaper onto a little table and went back to sitting in his chair, scowling at the street.

"I don't know," Penny continued as we started up the path to my grandpa's house, carefully avoiding Mr. Petrecelli's grass so he wouldn't come after *us* with his newspaper. "Maybe Dominic was just trying to help when he gave you the pencil case." I raised my eyebrows to say I seriously doubted that. "Anyway," she went on. "It doesn't matter. Just make the best project you can make, and don't worry about Dominic, okay?"

"Oh, I *will* make the best project," I answered, sounding more confident than I felt.

"I know you will," she said, and smiled as we pushed open my grandpa's front door. "You always make the coolest stuff. Like that thing you were doing today. I mean, until it thwacked Brianne in the head with a clothespin and then broke and got you in trouble. That looked amazing. What was it?"

"Oh, that?" I said, like it was nothing, even though it *had* been kind of inspired. "That was just a simple Rube Goldberg machine."

"Did I hear someone say 'Rube Goldberg'?" Grandpa came into the house through the back sliding doors and stopped at the sink to wash some gardening dirt off his hands.

Tomato, his dog, waddled in behind him, walked in two slow circles, and then sank down in his bed beside the couch. "You know, I met Rueben Goldberg once," Grandpa went on.

I knew.

So did Penny.

Telling people about the time he'd met the famous cartoonist and inventor in New York was one of Grandpa's favorite things to do. "Quite the gentleman," he began, "as sharp as a tack, and a real—"

"Barrel of monkeys," I finished for him. Grandpa put his hands on his hips and glared at me for interrupting his story, but I could tell he wasn't mad—not really.

"Who said I was talking to you, missy?" he joked. "I was telling my story to Penny here." Penny looked up from the floor where she'd plopped down beside Tomato's bed. She smiled, but only because she was way too polite to tell Grandpa that she'd also heard the Rube Goldberg story at least a hundred times.

"Back in the fifties Rube Goldberg was best known for the cartoons he drew," my grandpa began. "They featured machines that would perform a complicated series of movements to complete a simple task. Say you wanted to scratch Tomato's ears, like you're doing now," he explained. "You might get yourself the hand of a mannequin and attach it to a dowel, or a long stick." Grandpa's face was lit up, like it was every time he talked about Rube Goldberg machines. You could practically see the gears of his mind winding up and spinning in sync. "Then you could attach the end of the dowel to a spring, and above the spring you could position a small mallet to compress it. The pendulum of a ticking clock could be attached to a lever that would swing the mallet, compressing the spring and moving the mannequin hand up and down. And there you have it, a Rube Goldberg machine to pet your dog!"

"Or you could just sit here and use your hand," Penny said, giving Tomato a good scratch.

Grandpa laughed. "Or you could do that. But half the fun of a Rube Goldberg machine is watching it work in a complicated way to do something so simple."

"That's it!" Penny said suddenly. "Ruby! You should build a Rube Goldberg machine for your science project. I mean, you *are* named after the guy."

Grandpa blushed a little, probably remembering that Penny already knew his whole story about Rube Goldberg— including the part where he'd convinced my dad to name me after him—well, almost. I'd already had the Goldberg part, of course, and "Ruby" sounded a lot like "Rube."

Here's how *that* story goes: When I was just a few days old, I was waving my arms around while my mom was changing my diaper. One of my fingers got caught in the pull cord on the window blinds next to the change table. The blinds moved a little and tipped over a broom that was leaning up against the wall. When the broom fell, it knocked a small houseplant off the windowsill. At precisely that moment my dad was walking past with the laundry basket, and the falling plant surprised him so much that he dropped the whole thing onto his big toe. The shock of that made him hop around the room shouting, and he bumped into a lamp that crashed to the ground and broke.

"It was Ruby's roundabout way of telling her parents to turn the lights off already so she could get some sleep," Grandpa always finishes the story, laughing. "And I knew right then what we should name her.

"Well," Grandpa said now, changing the subject as he poured us glasses of lemonade. "I've got the game set up. Are you girls ready to play?"

We'd been having a Friday croquet tournament for the last month. Penny and I were tied with two wins each, although I had a feeling it was only because Grandpa was letting us win.

"Definitely," Penny said. "You're going down, Goldbergs."

"Oh, I doubt that, Penny Parker," I teased back. I was just about to close the sliding door behind us, when I noticed Tomato, still in his bed. "Toe-MAH-toe!" I said. It's what I called him when I was feeling fancy. "You coming, boy?"

Tomato loved to chase the croquet balls through the wickets. Sometimes Grandpa had to tie him up when the score was close, because otherwise he'd ruin the game. The dog opened his sad basset hound eyes and looked up at me mournfully, like he'd just lost his favorite chew toy and his heart was breaking into a billion pieces. Of course, that was how he *always* looked—even when he was happily chasing croquet balls or eating liver treats. But instead of leaping up on his stubby legs to trot after me, Tomato laid his head back down.

"He's a little out of sorts today," Grandpa said. "Maybe the heat." Grandpa walked over, bent down stiffly, and scratched Tomato in his favorite spot—right on the white patch on top of his head. "Poor guy," he said as Tomato looked up sadly. "It's tough getting old, isn't it? You can't get up and go like you used to. I know the feeling." Tomato lifted his head and pushed it into Grandpa's hand so he could get an even better scratch. "We'll check on him later," Grandpa told me. I bent down to give Tomato a scratch too.

"You're a good dog," I told him. "Yes, you are." I flopped his ears around a little—because they were just so floppable. Then I stood up, slid the patio door open, and went to kick some croquet butt.

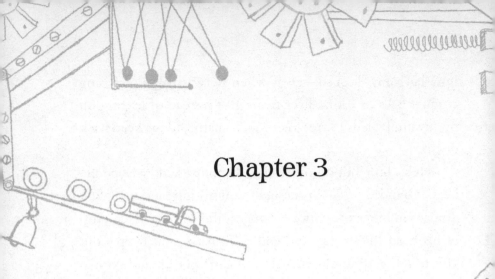

Chapter 3

In the end Grandpa won that day's croquet game, tying the tournament three ways.

"You know what this means . . . ," he said. "We'll have to keep playing."

Again, I couldn't prove anything, but I had a feeling he'd done that on purpose. My grandpa liked spending Fridays with me and Penny. And that was fine with me. I liked it too. The only problem was that it meant I always got home late, which meant that my sister Sarah was bound to have taken most of the pizza-night pepperonis.

"Mom!" I complained as I came into the kitchen and started to spread sauce on the mini pizza crust set out for me. "Sarah did it again."

"What?!" my sister exclaimed, taking yet another stack of pepperonis out of the package. "I need them for my pattern. It goes pepperoni, olive, pepperoni, red pepper." I looked at her pizza. It was perfect, almost like a flower, with the toppings arranged in a spiral that started in the center. But that didn't change the fact that it wasn't fair.

"Any particular reason the fridge is half full of balloons?" my mom asked casually. Her head was deep inside the refrigerator, where she was searching for the jar of hot peppers she and my dad liked to use. I'd had to move a few things around in there that morning to fit the balloons in, which explained why she couldn't find the jar. "Ruby?" she prompted.

"I'm exposing them to twelve hours of cold air," I said matter-of-factly. "Don't let me forget to measure their circumference after dinner." It was an experiment I'd found online about the effects of temperature on air pressure.

"There are a whole bunch on the floor in the living room too," Sarah reported. That was my "control" group, at room temperature. If anyone had used the basement bathroom that day, they would have noticed another bunch tied with strings to the grates of the heating vent in there where it was nice and warm.

My mom found her hot peppers and closed the fridge with a small sigh, leaving my balloons in place. Every now and then my experiments are not so convenient for my family—like when I used up all of my sister's school glue in my homemade slime experiment and forgot to tell her, or the time I tried to melt together toothpaste and Juicy Fruit gum to make my own anti-cavity gum, and it got so stuck to the bottom of the microwave that we had to get a new one. Mostly, though, my parents and Sarah just work around my experiments when they find them.

"Sarah," Mom said, eyeing my sister's pizza. "Share some pepperoni with your sister, okay?"

Sarah sighed, tossed her curly hair, and started picking the pepperoni off her pizza. "Fine," she said, putting them onto my plate. "I'll just make a new pattern." She reached for the bowl of pineapple chunks. I was sure that whatever she created next would be even nicer. My sister hardly ever did anything that wasn't perfect.

I chose a tomato slice and put it smack in the middle of my pizza like a giant clown nose, then plopped down some sliced olives for eyes.

"How was everyone's day?" Dad said, coming into the kitchen and taking the jar of hot peppers from Mom.

I was about to start telling my parents about the science fair and asking for their advice. Since Penny had suggested making a Rube Goldberg machine, I hadn't been able to get the idea out of my head, and I was definitely going to do it. I just wasn't sure what the machine would be for. All I knew was that it had to do something important if it was going to win me the gold. But before I could get a word in, as usual, my sister stole the spotlight.

"My day was great!" she said, grinning. "Actually . . ." She dusted her hands off and unzipped her backpack, which was lying on a chair. "I have something to show you." She presented Dad with a certificate.

"'The Rachel Halloway Lloyd Award for Excellence in Science—Eighth Grade!'" he read, holding it up. My sister was practically glowing with pride. Mom put aside her pizza and came over to see.

"Sarah, that's wonderful!" she said.

"I had a feeling I might win," Sarah admitted. "Since I'm getting top grades in science."

In science, and math, and language arts, and pretty much everything else! Don't get me wrong. As big sisters go, Sarah isn't that bad. She lets me have her old books—even the Roald Dahl ones that she still likes to read sometimes—and she always French braids my hair if I ask her. It's just that science is kind of my thing. And she's good at everything else. You'd think she could let me have that at least.

"And how was your day, Ruby?" Dad asked, seeming to remember I existed.

"Okay," I mumbled. I added a frowny green pepper mouth to my pizza face. "Pretty boring, I guess." Suddenly the fact that I was planning to do something amazing for my science fair project didn't seem like big news. At least not compared to the fact that my sister had *already done* something amazing.

And then everybody went right back to talking about

super-Sarah and her super science award. My mom even got out a bottle of sparkling cider and poured it into champagne glasses so we could make a toast before we ate our pizza.

"To a great scientific mind," Dad said. I clinked glasses with my family like I was supposed to, but I barely sipped at my cider. After all, I didn't have anything to celebrate. Not yet. And the less I told my family about the science fair, the better. That way, when I surprised them with the gold medal in a few short weeks, they'd be that much more impressed.

Or at least that had been my plan, but sometimes keeping secrets is harder than it seems—especially when you've got parents like mine, who are always paying attention.

"Ruby?" Dad said, coming up the stairs later that night. I was in the bathroom, standing on one foot while brushing my teeth and singing "Happy Birthday" three times in my head. Not that it was my triple birthday or anything. Dr. Coleman, our dentist, had just said to do that to make sure I brushed long enough—the "Happy Birthday" part, I mean. The standing on one foot part was my idea. It seemed like as good a time as any to practice improving my balance.

"I was taking your lunch bag out and I found this in your backpack." I looked at my dad's reflection in the mirror and saw that he was holding the science fair sign-up sheet. "It says here that you need to choose a topic by next Wednesday. Why didn't you mention this at dinner?"

"I munno," I mumbled, still brushing, still balancing. "Foogot." I could tell that my dad could tell that was a lie. I also knew he knew why I purposely "foogot." He'd probably noticed how quiet I'd been since Sarah had announced her big news. It was why he'd been asking me questions about school and making jokes all through dinner, trying to cheer me up.

"You know," Dad said, "your mom and I have always said that there could be two future scientists in this family. I'm not going to be surprised if we see the Rachel Halloway Lloyd Award for Excellence in Science coming home again when you get to eighth grade."

I switched feet, then I spat, then I rinsed, then I smiled. I knew that my parents hadn't been trying to hurt my feelings by making a big deal over Sarah's award. Still, I couldn't help thinking that I needed to prove myself.

"So," Dad went on. "I can't wait to hear what you've got planned this year, Miss Bronze and Silver Medalist."

"Well . . . ," I said, "I was thinking of a Rube Goldberg machine." Dad's eyes sparkled. He'd been hearing the stories about Rube Goldberg since *he* was a kid. He'd even come with me and Grandpa to MIT the year before to watch the judging of the Rube Goldberg Machine Design Contest. The winning machine had used thirty-five steps to put a stamp on an envelope.

"A Rube Goldberg machine! Now *that's* a great idea!" Dad said. "What's it going to do?"

"That's the only problem," I said. "I don't know. I want it to be something amazing. Something that no other Rube Goldberg machine has ever done before."

"Well . . ." Dad ruffled my hair, which totally threw me off balance. I had to grab the counter to steady myself. "With an inventor like you on the job, I have no doubt that, whatever it does, it will be something to see."

"I hope so," I said. Somehow the fact that he seemed so certain made me even more anxious. After all, the science fair was less than a month away, and aside from knowing that I wanted to make some kind of totally amazing Rube Goldberg machine, I didn't even have an idea yet!

The weekend came and went, and by Monday night I was no closer to finding my big idea. A machine that butters toast? Too small and insignificant! An automatic shoelace tier? Why not just wear Velcro shoes? A device that washes up the dinner dishes? Wait . . . they have that. It's called a dishwasher. "What am I," I sighed to myself, as I crossed yet another lame idea off my list, "some kind of amateur?"

"It'll come to you when you least expect it," my dad tried to reassure me. I hoped he was right. After dinner I went to the backyard to do a little spinning—something that usually clears my mind. I had just finished a really good twirl and was staggering toward the petunias, when my mom came outside.

"Ruby, sweetie?" she said. "I need to talk to you for a minute. You should probably sit down." She had that right.

Even though my feet had stopped, my head was still whirling, causing my mother, the backyard, and everything in it to tilt from side to side. I let myself fall on my butt, then lay down in the grass on my back, watching the sky revolve above me.

A few seconds later my mother's face came into focus enough that I could make out her worried expression.

"What's wrong?" I asked, propping myself up on my elbows.

"It's Tomato," she said.

I got a sinking feeling in my stomach. "Is he sick?" I remembered how he'd hardly moved from his bed when I'd seen him on Friday. But Grandpa had said it was probably the heat.

"No, honey. He died." My mom picked a clover out of the grass and squished it in her fingers as she talked. I could tell she was having trouble getting the words out. "When Grandpa woke up this morning, Tomato was dragging his back legs. Grandpa took him straight to the vet. He'd had a stroke. There was nothing they could do. They had to put him down."

"Oh," I said. It was all I could think of to say. I grabbed two big handfuls of grass and held on to them tightly, like I needed them to keep me from floating away. Tomato? Dead? It seemed impossible. Grandpa had had Tomato since before I was born. Wherever Grandpa went, he waddled close behind, his ears flip-flopping in time with his steps. He never left a shoe un-sniffed or a couch un-napped on.

I loved the way his soft, saggy skin flapped around when he ran after his blue and red ball . . . and the way he looked up at me with his big, sad eyes. I even loved the pond-water smell of the gross, sloppy dog kisses he gave. Grandpa's house was going to feel so strange without Tomato—and Grandpa, he was going to be so lonely!

"Can I go over and see Grandpa?" I asked. My mom looked up and smiled sadly.

"I think he'd like that," she said. "Dad can drive you when he's finished cleaning up the dinner dishes."

"That's okay," I said. "I'll ride my bike." It could take my dad nearly twenty minutes to load the dishwasher and wipe down the counters. I needed to see Grandpa right away to make sure he was okay.

I raced the six blocks to his house, my purple streamers flying in the wind, then threw my bike down on the lawn and ran up the path. I was just about to open the door when—

"A little common courtesy wouldn't hurt ya!"

I turned to see the neighbor, Mr. Petrecelli, leaning over his porch railing, waving his fly murdering newspaper in the general direction of my bike. "That's my lawn you're tossing your bike on. Where I'm from they call that trespassing!"

I didn't know where he was from—as far as I knew, Mr. Petrecelli had always lived right next door to my grandfather—but I did know that my bike was mostly on Grandpa's side of the lawn, and that, anyway, as crimes went, putting a bike on someone's grass was hardly serious.

Normally I would have apologized, but I was feeling so sad about Tomato. Couldn't Mr. Petrecelli give me a break for once? I stared at him hard, then walked back to my bike and nudged it over half an inch with my foot so it was even farther onto Grandpa's side.

"Happy?" I said.

Mr. Petrecelli looked anything but happy. "The insolence of young people today!" he announced to nobody in particular. I didn't know exactly what "insolence" meant, but if Mr. Petrecelli was saying it, it wasn't a compliment.

"The grumpiness of old people today!" I shot back. "Can't you ever just be nice? I would have moved my bike if you'd asked. And anyway, my grandpa's dog just died." I didn't know why I was bothering to tell Mr. Petrecelli that. If anything, he'd probably be glad, since it meant Tomato would never slip through the fence to pee on his prized poppies again. Still, Tomato was all I could think about, and I couldn't seem to keep the words in. "So if you want to talk about common courtesy, you should say you're sorry about our dog," I went on, "not yell about a bike that's barely even touching your stupid grass."

Mr. Petrecelli was in shock, I think. Even though we might be insolent (whatever that meant) pretty much every kid in the neighborhood was too afraid of him to ever talk back. I could tell it hadn't been a wise move either. His bottom lip started to quiver a little, like the biggest yell ever was about to burst out of his mouth. I turned and ran up the path, let myself in, and slammed Grandpa's door behind me before Mr. Petrecelli had the chance to start.

"Ruby? Is that you?" I followed Grandpa's voice into the living room, where I found him sitting in his favorite chair—the one with the footrest that pops out when you pull a lever. His eyes looked puffy and red, and he had a box of Kleenex beside him. I'd never seen my grandfather cry before, and it made me cry too.

"Come here," he said, holding out his arms. Even though I was technically too big for that kind of thing, I climbed into the chair and snuggled against him. "He was a good dog, wasn't he?" Grandpa said.

"I'm so sorry, Grandpa," I managed after a while.

"Me too," he answered. "But it's okay." He rested his chin against the top of my head. "Tomato had thirteen good years with our family. And if he hadn't made us so happy, we wouldn't be feeling so sad right now, would we?"

I hadn't thought about it that way before, but it was true. Sadness and happiness were mixed up like that. You couldn't have one without the other.

Just then I heard a familiar jangling noise and looked up, my heart full of hope. Grandpa smiled sadly. "It's just Tomato's collar," he said, showing me the blue leather loop. He'd been clutching it in one hand, but I hadn't noticed before.

"You biked over here in a real hurry. You must be thirsty. How about some lemonade?" Grandpa said. I climbed out of the chair. Then Grandpa pushed the lever that snapped the footrest back into place, stood up, and slid Tomato's collar into his pocket. "Then maybe you can tell me about your latest ideas for the science fair," he went on.

So we drank some lemonade, and we made another list of ideas (none of which were much better than a toast-butterer or automatic dishwasher), and I told Grandpa about the Roald

Dahl book I was reading (where this boy climbs inside a giant peach with talking caterpillars and things), and we carried on like things were mostly normal—even though they weren't, and both of us kept glancing over at Tomato's empty bed.

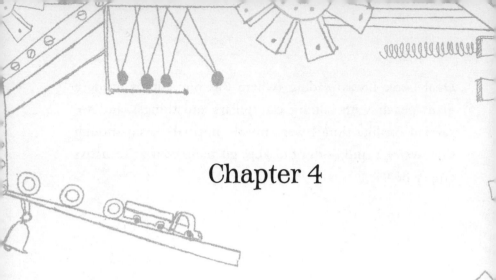

Chapter 4

I had a hard time sleeping that night. I kept thinking about Grandpa, alone without Tomato to keep his feet warm in bed—which maybe explains why I was exhausted and just a little bit on edge by the time I got to school the next day.

"Hey, Ruby."

Even if I hadn't been in a particularly cranky mood, being greeted in the school yard first thing by Dominic Robinson would have been the last thing I needed. "Just one day left to choose science fair topics," he chirped—like I would have forgotten! Besides Grandpa and Tomato, it was practically all I could think about. "Do you have an idea yet?"

"Maybe," I said. I still knew I was going to build a Rube Goldberg machine, but I wasn't any closer to figuring out what it would do yet—plus, I had *no* intention of telling Dominic anything and having him copy my idea *again*.

"I'm thinking of hatching baby chicks," he said, "and studying how they break out of their eggs. That is, if my dad's friend can lend me an incubator."

Baby chicks? The cuteness factor alone would put him into the top three. That was *so unfair!*

It took every ounce of willpower I had not to tell him that I was going to do *something even better* than that. If I could only figure out exactly what my machine was going to do. But then I had an idea. . . .

"Sounds neat, I guess," I said, giving him a smug smile. "Personally, I'm probably going to stick with a classic. The baking-soda-and-vinegar volcano." Dominic looked confused for a second, then he half smiled, like he wasn't sure if I was joking. Penny walked up with her fingers hooked underneath her backpack straps. "I've already started, actually," I added. "Penny's been helping me."

Obviously she was confused, so I filled her in. "With my volcano, right, Penny? For the science fair? I'm making it out of papier-mâché. It's going to be a to-scale model of Mount Saint Helens. When I'm done, it'll be so big that it will almost touch the ceiling in the gym."

Penny nodded a little too enthusiastically, catching on to my plan to mislead Dominic. "Oh, yeah," she said. "The volcano! It's going to be awesome."

"Really?" Dominic said, like he still didn't quite believe it.

"What's wrong with that?" I said in my most offended tone.

"Nothing. It's just . . . a volcano? I guess I thought you'd do something really *interesting*."

"For your information, when Mount Saint Helens erupted, it was the largest known debris avalanche in recorded history." I knew, because my dad and I had watched a show about in on the Discovery Channel the night before. "And that's *very interesting*," I added.

I huffed at Dominic, then Penny huffed at him, and then, in perfect sync, we turned our backs and huffed away together. "Do you think he bought it?" Penny whispered when we were far enough away.

"I hope so," I whispered back. But even if he hadn't, at least now I had the advantage. Dominic didn't have a clue what I'd really be doing—but I knew *exactly* what I was up against. And clearly I had my work cut out for me. I had just one day left to come up with an idea that would beat a pile of fluffy, peeping baby chicks. "Think, Ruby, think!" I urged my brain. I was starting to feel desperate and panicky, and I knew I needed to boost my confidence.

"Penny?" I asked. "How do you say 'kick butt' in American Sign Language?"

She held up one hand, then karate chopped it with the other from underneath. "That's kick," she said. "They never taught 'butt' at my sign language class. How about 'bottom'? That's what my grandma calls it."

"Okay. Close enough," I said, and I copied the second sign she showed me, touching the base of one palm with the side of the other.

"I don't know how yet," I said, practicing the signs again, "but, baby chicks or no baby chicks, this is exactly what I'm planning to do in the science fair."

Penny smiled, made a fist, and nodded it at me, signing "Yes."

Then later that day—just like my dad had promised it would—my big idea came to me when I was least expecting it. It happened after school.

I waved at Penny as her mom drove her away for sign language class, then I hopped onto my bike and rode straight to Grandpa's. Thankfully, Mr. Petrecelli was nowhere in sight, but just to be on the safe side, I was careful to wheel my bike to the side of the house, where I propped it up using the kickstand. Then I went around the front to let myself in. That morning's newspaper was still sitting on the doorstep, rolled up in one of the thick pink elastic bands the paperboy uses. There was also a small plant, with bright blue paper wrapped around it, the exact color of Tomato's collar. A note card was attached to it. *Sorry for your loss,* it read. There wasn't any signature.

"Grandpa?" I said, pushing open the door and carrying the plant and newspaper inside.

"In here!" he called. I found him in the living room,

where he was busy lifting off the sofa cushions, looking for something.

"You forgot to get your paper," I said, putting the *Somerville Times* down on the coffee table.

"Oh. So I did!" He shook his head. "Tomato always used to bring it in."

"And somebody left you this." I held up the plant. He took it from me and read the card.

"Well, isn't that nice. I wonder who it could be from. Hang on a second and I'll get it some water. I just need to find my slippers. I can't think where I put them."

Fetching Grandpa's slippers had been another of Tomato's jobs, I realized. He also used to eat the crumbs off the kitchen floor and bark every time somebody rang the doorbell, to make sure that Grandpa had heard it.

"I guess I'll have to get used to getting my own paper and slippers," Grandpa said sadly. "For now, anyway. Maybe someday I'll get another dog. But I just don't know. As nice as another dog might be, he just won't be Tomato."

While Grandpa continued to pull off the sofa cushions, I checked on the floor behind a pile of magazines, then next to the big potted fern. The slippers were nowhere in sight.

More than anything I wished Tomato were still alive. Not only had he been Grandpa's faithful friend, but I hadn't realized how much of a help he'd been around the house. If only there were a way I could do something to make life easier for Grandpa—

And that was the moment it clicked into place. If I could build some sort of contraption that brought in Grandpa's paper and fetched his slippers, he wouldn't need to worry about those things anymore. And . . . since I'd been planning to build a Rube Goldberg machine for the science fair anyway . . . why not make one that did exactly those things? Forget buttering toast and tying shoelaces. I could do something important by helping Grandpa feel better about losing Tomato, *and* I could win the gold medal and show Dominic and his fluffy baby chicks a thing or two!

When I closed my eyes, I could practically see the name of my machine spelled out in lights: The Tomato-Matic 2000. It would start with a scale that I'd place underneath the doormat, which would get triggered when the paperboy tossed the *Somerville Times* on top of it. From there a pulley system would be activated, scooping up the paper in a wicker basket, but would that hold? I forced myself to stop there. I'd work out the details later. The most important thing was to get started.

"Grandpa!" I said breathlessly. "I think I just came up with an amazing idea for my science project. But it's going to be big. I'll need space to put it together. Can I use your shed?"

"What's that?" Grandpa said. He'd abandoned his search under the sofa cushions and was looking for his slippers on the floor near the shelves where he kept his model planes. "You want to use the shed? Sure thing, Ruby. It's yours. Just move the paint cans over if you need to."

It was weird that Grandpa hadn't even asked what my project was going to be about, but then again, I could see how distracted he was without Tomato at his side. It was all the more reason I needed to take action, and fast!

"It's going to be a surprise, though, okay?" I said. "So don't come back there until I say so."

"Okay, Ruby," he said. "If you need anything, just say the word." I promised that I would. Then I ran out the back door and toward the shed in such a frenzy that I almost crashed right into Mr. Petrecelli, who was—I would just like to point out—trespassing on my grandfather's lawn.

He was standing near a white wooden cross I'd never seen before. My first thought was that it must have been some kind of marker that Grandpa had put in for our croquet game, but then I realized, with a sick feeling, what it actually was: a little grave near the fence that separated Grandpa's yard from Mr. Petrecelli's. Grandpa hadn't told me that he'd buried Tomato back there.

Mr. Petrecelli shuffled his feet. "Mind you don't go knocking that over," he barked at me, using his cane to point at the cross. "And keep off the flowers if you're going to go traipsing around back here." Then, before I could even get a word in, he turned and walked back into his house, slamming the screen door behind him.

I shook my head, but I didn't let it faze me. After all, I had more important things to think about than some grumpy old man.

"Don't worry, Tomato" I said softly, stopping in front of the little cross. "Grandpa misses you, but I'll make sure he's okay. I've just thought of the greatest way to cheer him up." And then I ran the rest of the way, let myself into the shed, and got started on my machine.

Chapter 5

"Mooooooommm! My shoelaces are missing!"

A little more than a week had gone by, and the Tomato-Matic 2000 was already coming together nicely, if I did say so myself. The only problem was that I was running a little short on supplies.

"What do you mean your shoelaces are missing?" Mom called back to Sarah from the bottom of the stairs. "Aren't they in your shoes?"

"They were," Sarah said. She came down holding out her red Converse. I ducked my head and pretended to be completely absorbed in putting my books into my backpack. "I'm also missing half the hangers in my closet. And I can't find my dangly earrings. The ones with the rhinestones."

I crumpled the top of my red file folder in my hurry to get my bag zipped, but it didn't matter. Getting out the door undetected with my supplies was the most important thing. It was just my luck that Sarah would have noticed the shoelaces. She hadn't worn those Converse in months. And as for the clothes hangers, there hadn't been any clothes hanging on them. So it wasn't like she'd been using them, technically.

"I saw those earrings in the bathroom yesterday," my mom said. "But I have no idea where your shoelaces would be. Are you sure you didn't take them out for some reason and then forget?"

"Why would I take out my shoelaces?"

I put on my own shoes—which were also missing their laces—and was almost at the door, when one of my shoes slipped off and I wobbled and tripped, dropping my bag. It landed with a huge thud. Mom turned, glanced at my runaway shoe and then at my schoolbag. "Ruby?" she asked. "Where are *your* shoelaces?"

"They, um, broke," I said. It was true. I'd needed them to suspend the wicker basket from the clothesline, where it would catch the newspaper that got catapulted up by the weight of a bowling ball falling onto a teeter-totter . . . but I hadn't been counting on how old my laces were. One of them had snapped almost immediately, and after two trial runs the second one was already wearing thin—which was why I needed to borrow Sarah's.

"And did you happen to take the laces from your sister's shoes to replace them?" Mom asked.

"Well . . . ," I said, trying to buy myself time to think of a way to bend the truth. But it was too late. I'd hesitated, and my mom was onto me.

"I'd like you to give them back, please," she said. I sighed, opened my backpack, and pulled the laces out . . . but I guess I hadn't stuffed everything in quite firmly enough, because with the laces came a bunch of colorful binder clips that I'd taken from my mom's desk drawer. They skittered across the tile floor.

"Ruby!" Mom said, bending over to pick them up. "Are these my clips?" I didn't answer. "I need these for my case files."

"I think she has my hangers, too," Sarah said, catching sight of one of the metal hooks that was sticking out of the top of my bag now.

"Okay, Ruby," Mom said, putting her hands on her hips. "Everything out, please."

I pouted, but I started to unpack.

I took out the rest of the binder clips and hangers, then added a few other things to the pile: the rubber mat we usually keep near the back door for boots, a ruler from my dad's workshop, and the coiled-up clothesline cable from our yard. (I needed a pulley system, and my parents hardly ever had time to hang out the laundry, anyway.)

"There," I said.

Mom and Sarah looked at each other, and then at me. "All of it," they said together.

I sighed and unzipped my backpack all the way.

I took out some old Hot Wheels tracks and half the marbles from our Chinese checkers game, two rolls of masking tape, a paintbrush, a package of party balloons, plus a jumbo jar of peanut butter and a box of crackers. (A girl's got to eat, right?)

Mom handed the shoelaces and hangers back to Sarah. "You know we want to support you with your science project," she said. "But you can't keep taking things from the house without asking. We might need this." She held up the clothesline and eyed it, like she was trying to remember exactly what it was for. "Here." She reached for her purse and pulled a crisp twenty-dollar bill out of her wallet. "That's all I've got for now. Why don't you stop by the hardware store after school and get whatever you need?" I nodded, taking the bill from her.

"Thanks. Can I at least keep the peanut butter?" I asked.

Mom cracked a small smile. "That, I think we can spare, *if* you can apologize to your sister."

"Sorry, Sarah," I mumbled.

"Just don't do it again," she answered, then sat down on the steps and started to rethread her laces.

"Fine," I said, even though I wasn't 100 percent sure I could keep that promise. Twenty dollars was a lot of money—and it wasn't that I didn't appreciate my parents' help—but if

I wanted to make the best machine possible, I was going to need *a lot* of stuff. And, anyway, what was the big deal about borrowing some old shoelaces and a few wire hangers when it was all in the name of science?

Thankfully, the minor supplies shortage aside, it seemed that luck was finally on my side. We were in line for long jump in gym class that day, when I overheard Dominic talking to his friend Peter. The week before, Ms. Slate had called a bunch of kids to the front of the room to talk about their science projects—and now I knew why!

"That's dumb," Peter was saying. "Like it's your fault that Tammy's trained rats escaped last year and one of them crawled up Mrs. Daniel's leg! Even if your baby chicks *did* escape in the gym, what's the worst they're going to do? Peep at someone?"

"I know," Dominic answered, sounding a little defeated. "But I guess the teachers can't let kids use one kind of live animal for science fair projects and not another. It wouldn't be fair. Anyway," he added as the line moved up, "it's okay. I have another idea, even though it's not as good."

In a lot of ways I had to agree with Peter. It was dumb that Ms. Slate and the other teachers had decided to ban projects that used live animals just because of a few escaped rats. I mean, there's so much we can learn from watching small mammals and reptiles! Still, I couldn't stop myself from smiling. Now that the cuddly baby chicks had been banned, there was nothing standing in my way of the gold medal. That is, if I could just get the catapult part of the machine right. Half the time when the newspaper landed on one side of the catapult, it triggered the bowling ball to release, which launched the newspaper into the waiting basket. But the other half of the time, the *Somerville Times* missed the basket completely and knocked over the rake Grandpa kept in the corner, which bounced against the stack of snow tires, tipped over some empty paint cans, and scared the squirrels that were stealing sunflower seeds from the bird feeder outside the window—hardly the chain reaction I'd been going for!

"I'm really starting to get nervous now," Penny said. "But you'll be there next Saturday afternoon for the dress rehearsal, right? And then next Sunday night for the show? I need you right in the front row where I can see you."

What? Be where? I realized all of a sudden that Penny, who was standing in line behind me, had been talking for a while, but I'd been so busy eavesdropping on Dominic and Peter and thinking about my machine that I'd managed to miss most of what she'd said.

"Of course!" I said, even though I wasn't exactly sure what I was agreeing to. "Front row."

"Thanks." Penny smiled. "I'll dance so much better if I can see a friendly face. Plus, that way you'll have a close-up view of my costume. My mom's almost finished with the peacock feather headband. It looks pretty cool."

"The peacock dance!" I exclaimed, finally figuring out what we were talking about. "Where you make peacock hands. Of course. I can't wait to see it. Does it look kind of like this?" I made pointy beak shapes with both my hands and waved them around over my head.

"No." Penny laughed. "Sorry . . . but that looks more like the drowning chicken dance."

"No way! *This* is the drowning chicken dance." I stuck my hands into my armpits and flapped my elbows as fast as possible, like I was trying to stay afloat. Then I added a panicked pecking motion with my neck and started to bend my knees, sinking to the floor like I was going underwater. "Bok, bok, bok, bok, BOOOOOK." I added freaked-out chicken sounds to make it extra realistic.

"Um . . . ," Penny said, then she burst out laughing. "It's unique . . . but I don't think you're ready for a recital yet."

"Oh, please. You're just jealous of my style," I teased. Brianne, Ally, and a couple of other girls were leaning out of the line and giving me weird looks, so I stopped dancing. I was glad I'd made Penny smile, but most of the kids in the class were still mad at me about the Hershey's Kisses incident. They already didn't like me very much, and I didn't need to give them more of a reason to talk about me.

The line moved up again. We were five people from the beginning, and now that I was done chicken dancing, I started to wonder how on earth I was going to get past Mr. Trellis, the gym teacher, and manage to land a long jump with no laces in my shoes. My sneakers had been falling off all day just from regular walking.

"Hey," I said, eyeing Penny's shoelaces. They were nice strong thick ones with happy-face designs on them. She'd just gotten them a few weeks before too, so they were clean and strong. Come to think of it, they'd be perfect for suspending the newspaper basket in my Rube Goldberg machine! "Do you think I could borrow one of your shoelaces for the long jump?" I asked.

"Sure," she said, bending down and starting to unlace it.

"Thanks!" I said. Then I added, "And maybe I could keep it for a few weeks? It's for my science project," I explained quickly when she raised her eyebrows. "I was going to borrow Sarah's, but my family doesn't want me using their stuff anymore."

Penny sighed a little. It wasn't the first time I'd asked to borrow her things for science-related reasons. There was the time I'd needed her sandwich container to collect worms in . . . the time she'd lent me her favorite sparkly ponytail elastic to build a high-powered slingshot . . . the day I'd accidentally sunk her Thermos to the bottom of the pond while doing a floatability experiment. For a second I thought I might be out of luck, but then Penny laughed and held the shoelace up to me. "Of course. If you need it."

"Thanks," I said.

"No problem." She shrugged. "You know I'll do anything I can do to help you." I could have hugged her. Even if my family didn't seem to want to help me out much, at least I knew I could always count on my best friend.

And I was even more grateful for Penny and her happy-face shoelace that day after school when I got to the hardware store. You can say what you want about scientific work, but it sure isn't cheap! Did you know that a clothesline kit alone costs $14.49 plus tax? With my mom's twenty dollars and some loose change I found in my backpack, I barely had enough to cover that, some wood screws, a small tin of floor wax, and a little key chain with a pig on it that was on sale for $2.99. When you pressed a button on its back, it oinked at you and its nose lit up. And, okay, maybe I didn't technically *need* it for my machine, but it was so cute! How was I supposed to resist?

Now I just had to hope that Grandpa would let me borrow a plastic mat to put underneath the catapult to hold it steady, and that he had some spare binder clips lying around.

I was at the checkout, counting out my last few cents, when I saw Dominic and his dad. They were walking toward the cash register with a basket brimming with stuff. Gears, wires, carbon rods, ball bearings, and epoxy glue. I gulped. Baby chicks would have been worse, don't get me wrong, but this still looked serious.

"You might want some crazy glue for the rotor head," Dominic's dad said. "Wait in line. I'll be right back."

For a second I thought I might be able to slip out the

door undetected, but just as I was about to make a run for it, Dominic turned and saw me.

"Oh, hey, Ruby," he said. "Just stocking up on a few things for my science project." *That* was an understatement. He was buying half the store! "What are you doing?" he asked.

"Oh, you know," I tried to act casual. "Same."

He gave me a strange look. "Why do you need a clothes-line for a giant volcano?"

"Oh, this?" I hugged the package I was holding against my chest. "This is for my . . . clothes. To, ummm . . ."

"You're not building a model of Mount Saint Helens, are you?" he said. "I knew it! I knew you were just keeping your idea secret. You're probably doing something way cooler. I'm not allowed to do the baby chicks anymore," he went on. "Ms. Slate says live animals are against the rules this year. So I'm just building an RC helicopter instead." He held up his basket to show me the parts.

Just a remote controlled helicopter? Building something that was *actually* going to fly, *completely* from scratch, was *totally* amazing.

"That sounds kind of cool," I said, remaining aloof.

"I guess. It just doesn't seem that important, you know? Lots of people have done it before." Dominic shrugged. "But who knows. Maybe I'll discover something new along the way. Like how the chemist who invented Post-it notes was trying to make a superstrong glue, but he messed up the batch and made something cooler. That's the great thing about science, right? You never know when you might discover something."

I wasn't about to admit it out loud, but I actually agreed with Dominic there. (Also, I'd never heard that story about Post-it notes before. I was definitely going to look it up online when I got home.) It really *was* true. The next big scientific breakthrough could always be right around the corner. It was exactly that possibility that made me keep filling the fridge with balloons, experimenting with the fizzy antibacterial tablets my sister used to clean her retainer, and hiding old potatoes around my room to see if I could find the optimal level of darkness to make them grow more eyes. (My mom had yet to discover *that* little experiment . . . but it was starting to smell a little funny, so it wouldn't be long.)

I could hardly believe that—for once—Dominic and I actually had the same opinion on something. *But wait a second* . . . I stopped myself. Was he serious, or was he just trying to act friendly to get my defenses down? And why was he telling me his new project idea, anyway? If I hadn't been able to see the helicopter parts, right there in his basket, I might have suspected he was lying to me, like I'd lied to him about the volcano. I narrowed my eyes at him, but he didn't seem to notice.

"For a while I was thinking about making a Rube Goldberg machine—like the ones you're always making at your desk, but I didn't know if I'd be very good at it. I've never tried before."

Was this Dominic's way of hinting that he already knew my idea? The only person I'd told, besides my family, was Penny, and I knew she'd never tell. Unless Dominic had been sneaking around, listening in on our conversations!

"How did you know?" I said. I hadn't meant to say it, but the words came out anyway, angry and accusing.

Dominic looked confused.

"How did you know I was making a Rube Goldberg machine?" I added.

"You are?" Dominic's face brightened. "I didn't know that! I can't believe we almost had the same idea. That's so great!"

"Great" wasn't exactly the word I would have used. I could have kicked myself. Now that Dominic knew what I was doing, it would be that much easier for him to beat me—or worse, copy me again.

"You always come up with awesome ideas, Ruby. I don't think I ever told you, but when I heard you were making a citrus clock, that's what inspired me to build my potato-powered grandfather clock last year, so I kind of owe you. . . ."

Oh! I'd *inspired* him! Well, *that* was a fancy way of admitting that he'd stolen my idea.

"Hey . . . if you need any help . . ." He trailed off. "I've always wanted to try making a Rube Goldberg machine."

Dominic's help was the *last* thing I needed. Let him in to see my entire project so he could learn all the details and use them against me? No, thanks!

"My dad knows the owner here, so he gets a discount. I could chip in for supplies. And we could even use my helicopter as part of your machine if you want."

So now he was trying to bribe me with free stuff? I knew better than to fall for that trick. Still, an RC helicopter would open up a whole world of possibilities. Like, maybe when the newspaper landed on the coffee table near Grandpa's chair, it could trigger a second sensor that would launch the helicopter, which could pick up Grandpa's slippers and carry them across the room. We could even paint the words "Tomato Copter" on the side of it. I could already imagine it whizzing efficiently across the room. I shook my head, trying to snap myself out of it. Helicopter or no helicopter, I was *not* going to let Dominic help with my project. It wasn't worth the risk. Anyway, my parents would help me buy supplies if I really needed them.

Dominic smiled innocently, pushed his overgrown hair out of his eyes, and set his basket down near the cash register. "Think about it, okay?" he said, emptying all the stuff onto the counter. There must have been a hundred dollars' worth of supplies! "If you want," he went on, "we could even pair up. Supeng and Eleni asked if they could do a group project this year, and Ms. Slate said it was okay. Plus, you've won bronze and silver and I've won gold. We'd make a pretty unstoppable team," he added.

A team? Yeah, right! That was the craziest thing I'd ever heard.

But then it hit me: If we *did* work together on a single project, there was no way that Dominic could beat me, was there? Plus, wasn't there an expression . . . keep your friends close, but your enemies closer? I didn't love the idea of having Dominic by my side, but maybe it wouldn't be so bad. At least that way I could watch his every move.

"I'll think about it," I said, eyeing Dominic suspiciously. "But no promises."

Dominic grinned like I'd just promised him the moon. "Okay," he said.

The whole way to Grandpa's house, I wondered if, by even just agreeing to think it over, I'd made the biggest mistake ever.

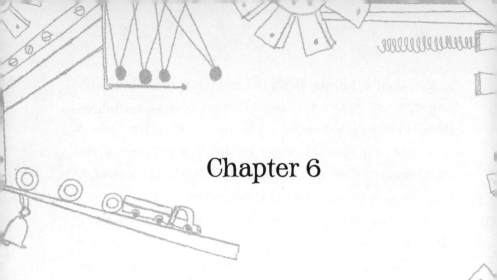

Chapter 6

That afternoon and evening I didn't watch cartoons or read a single chapter of my Roald Dahl book. I didn't start any new inventions or experiments at home (even though after I confirmed my hypothesis about how to grow a potato with maximum eyes, I was dying to find out if I'd get the same results with yams). Instead I spent all my time in Grandpa's shed, working on the Tomato-Matic 2000, and one thing started to become painfully obvious: I needed help.

"Ouch!" I said, for what felt like the millionth time, as the basket holding the newspaper rolled partway up the clothesline, stopped, swung around wildly, and hit me on the head. I'd tried greasing the clothesline with floor wax, then I'd tried making the line shorter . . . then tighter, but no matter what I did, the newspaper was just too heavy to go the whole distance.

Finally I got the idea to attach one end of the clothesline way up high on the garage wall so that it angled down sharply, letting gravity do the work. That did the trick! The only problem was that it worked too well. On my first trial the basket went flying down the clothesline at high speed. When it reached the end, the newspaper shot out, sailed straight through the shed window, which was—thankfully—open, and landed smack in the middle of Grandpa's birdbath, nearly giving a cardinal a heart attack. I felt so bad that I went outside and tried to feed the bird a snack that Penny had given me to taste test—some kind of sticky granola and raisin stuff in a baggy. It was pretty delicious, but I think the poor thing was too much in shock to eat. To sum it up, things were *not* going well.

"That looks like it's coming along," my dad said that night as he peered over my shoulder. It was past bedtime, but I was still working on sketches at the dining room table, trying to figure out a way to keep the newspaper in the basket. So far I'd thought of wrapping it in Saran wrap or securing it with Velcro fasteners. Both ideas would keep the paper out of the birdbath, but they'd make it next to impossible to dump it when it reached the end of the line—and getting the newspaper onto Grandpa's coffee table was the whole point.

"Not really," I said miserably, rubbing out the Velcro fasteners with my eraser. "I can't make this part work." I explained the flying newspaper problem to my dad.

"What if you didn't angle the clothesline so much?" he suggested.

"I've tried that. But the newspaper is too heavy. If I don't use the force of gravity, it won't work." I rubbed at my forehead and stared at the drawing again, trying to see it with fresh eyes. "Maybe I should just give up and build a stupid baking soda volcano after all," I said.

"Come on. You don't mean that," Dad said. "The Ruby Goldberg I know never gives up that easily."

He was right, of course. I didn't mean it. I was just frustrated, and tired.

"You know . . ." he said, pulling up a chair. "When gravity alone won't do the trick, a little horsepower often comes in handy. Why don't you put in a motor?" He took the pencil from me and started to sketch a coil sort of thing near the top of the clothesline. "Kind of like this," he said.

It looked simple enough on paper.

"But I don't know anything about motors," I pointed out. "And the science fair is barely two weeks away. I don't think I have time to learn."

"You know . . . it's funny," Dad said. "I was having that same problem at work today. Bonnie asked me to turn in a report on acquisitions and our new profit sharing model." I nodded, trying to pretend like I wasn't about to fall asleep.

"It's due next week, and I'm no expert on profit sharing—so you know what I did?"

I shrugged and looked up from my sketch quickly, trying to act slightly interested so I wouldn't hurt my dad's feelings.

"I got Tanya in accounting to do it for me."

"DAD!" I shouted. "You got someone else to do your work for you? That's cheating!"

Dad laughed. "It's not cheating. It's working together. I'm still writing the part about acquisitions, since that's what I know best, and Tanya's writing about the new model, since she's the expert. In the end we'll have a better report than if I'd done it alone. It's the same as when your mom and I help each other with the Sunday crossword. Two minds are better than one, don't you think? And that's especially true when it comes to scientific discovery."

He had my attention now.

"Have you heard of Banting and Best? They invented insulin together, and that saved the lives of thousands of people with diabetes. Or how about the Wright brothers? It took two great minds to get that plane off the ground!" He paused. "Or take Ben & Jerry. Do you think one person alone could have dreamed up something as delicious as triple chocolate brownie fudge explosion ice cream?"

"Dad!" I said, rolling my eyes at his silly example. Then I bit at my thumbnail while I gave the matter some thought. I hated to admit it, but maybe he was right. I still didn't trust Dominic . . . but I could definitely use his skills—and there was no telling how great the machine could be if we worked together. Plus, like I'd said before, if he was my partner, at least I could keep a close eye on him. "Well . . . ," I admitted. "There's this one person in my class who wants to work with me. And he *is* pretty good at things like motors."

"There you go, then!" My dad grinned, as if the solution were that simple. "Now let's get your great scientific mind off to bed."

But even though I slept on the decision, I didn't wake up feeling any more certain. If we did work as partners, could I trust Dominic to do his best and not sabotage the project? Would his helicopter be strong enough to lift Grandpa's slippers? Would I be able to stand the turtlelike look of him peering out from underneath his bangs every single afternoon until the science fair started?

All morning long I hemmed and hawed, but the truth was, I knew I needed Dominic. So at silent reading time I propped my book open in front of me to act as a privacy screen. Then I pulled the tiny spring out of a ballpoint pen and quietly taped it to a piece of stiff cardboard I'd snatched from the recycle bin on my way into class. I tested it once, then wrote my answer on a note, folded it into a tiny square, and pressed it down against the mini catapult. *SPROINGGGG.* The square of paper sailed across the aisle and landed smack in the middle of Dominic's desk, exactly like I'd planned.

"Ahhh!" he screamed, jumping in his seat. Now, that part I hadn't planned. The whole class, including Ms. Slate, turned to look at Dominic. I shook my head in disgust. What was the point of building a spring-loaded-secret-note-passing machine if the person receiving the note couldn't even keep quiet?

"Is everything okay, Dominic?" Ms. Slate asked.

"Oh, yeah," Dominic said. "Just this tiny paper . . . um . . . paper cut." He held up a finger. "Sorry." A few kids at the front snickered, but then everyone went back to reading. Dominic quietly unfolded my note and read it. Then he leaned across the aisle. "What do you mean by 'Okay!'?" he asked in a loud whisper.

I sighed softly. I ask you, would I have taken the time to pass him a note if I'd wanted to whisper back and forth across the aisle?

"Okay!" I whispered back, giving up. "It means, okay. I thought about it, and you can help with my Rube Goldberg machine. We can be partners. Come to my Grandpa's house with me after school tomorrow. Bring your helicopter."

I went back to my silent reading book—*Charlie and the Chocolate Factory*. I was just at the part where Charlie finds the golden ticket, when, *WHOOSH*, something sailed right in front of my nose and landed on my lap. "Wha—" I said, pushing my chair back in surprise. Penny looked at me from across the room, and Ally and Brianne turned in their seats. Thankfully, Ms. Slate was busy writing the homework on the board, and if she'd heard me, she was choosing to ignore it.

I grabbed the square of paper and unfolded it quickly. *Okay!!* it read.

I glanced across the aisle just in time to see Dominic putting away the note launcher he'd built with two rulers, a rubber band, and a stack of textbooks. It was basic, at best, but

I had to give him points for trying, and I couldn't help notic-
ing: He was grinning like a five-year-old on his birthday.

But as happy as Dominic seemed in class, the look on his face
was nothing compared to how overjoyed he was the next day
at Grandpa's house.

"Hello?" I called out. I'd picked up the newspaper again
on our way in and was carrying it under one arm, along with
the mail. The letter carrier always came first thing in the
morning, which meant that Grandpa hadn't left the house
all day. Without Tomato to take for walks, I guessed he didn't
have much of a reason to get outside. It worried me. So did
the dishes piled on the kitchen counter, and the grass in the
front yard that hadn't been mowed in almost two weeks and
was creeping up past my calves. "I'm here!" I called again.
"And I brought someone with me."

"Just a second. I'll be right out." Grandpa's voice was
coming from the bedroom. It wasn't like him to take a nap in
the middle of the afternoon, but then again he hadn't exactly
been acting like himself since Tomato had died.

"You can put your bag down there." I showed Dominic
the spot on the floor where I always dropped my backpack.
"I'll get us something to drink."

"Cool!" Dominic exclaimed, walking to the far side of
the living room and inspecting the display case Grandpa
kept there. It was lined top to bottom with the model
planes he used to build. My favorite was a little yellow and

black one called the Champ. I wasn't so much into planes, but I'd helped Grandpa build it when I was seven. He'd put it together, and then I'd painted it. "Are these all your grandfather's?"

"I see you found my planes," Grandpa said before I had the chance to answer. He was coming down the last few stairs, holding tight to the banister. "Ruby and I built one of those together." It made me feel proud that he'd remembered. "I'm Alfred," Grandpa said. "And you are?"

"Dominic, sir," he answered. "I'm helping Ruby with her science project. Do they really fly?" he asked, turning his attention back to the planes. I could see his reflection in the pane of glass. His eyes seemed to grow wider and wider with each plane he studied.

"The ones on the top row do," Grandpa said, coming up behind him to point them out. "All except that one there."

"The P-47D Thunderbolt!" Dominic exclaimed.

"A boy who knows his planes." Grandpa sounded impressed. "She's a beauty. The engine gave out a few years back, though. And my hands are a little shaky these days. I don't think I'd be able to fix it."

"I could fix it for you." Dominic dug his hands deep into his pockets. "If you wanted me to. I made a Super Cub DSM before . . . and my dad helped me with a Firebird Commander last year. That one was hard."

"Well, isn't that something?" Grandpa was smiling. "I've

got a Firebird in my collection too. As I remember, installing the sensors was tricky."

"Dominic's building an RC helicopter," I announced. "All from parts from the hardware store. It's not even a kit." I was surprised to hear myself bragging about Dominic's accomplishments, but I hadn't seen Grandpa looking so happy in weeks. Maybe talking to someone about model planes was just the thing he needed to help him feel a little less sad about Tomato—at least until the Tomato-Matic 2000 was ready for its grand unveiling.

Grandpa slid the glass of the cabinet open and lifted out the Thunderbolt. It was definitely one of the nicest planes—a deep forest green with a checkerboard pattern on the nose and wingtips. "It's not every day I have an expert model builder come to visit and offer his services," Grandpa said. "She's yours if you're willing to fix her."

"You mean . . . ?" Dominic's eyes were positively enormous now.

"If you can get her flying, you can keep her," Grandpa said. "She's not doing much good sitting in that case. Just bring her by so I can take her for a spin when she's ready."

Dominic took the little plane from Grandpa, holding it so carefully you'd think it was made of glass.

"This is *so* awesome!" he said.

"Come on, Dominic." I held out a glass of lemonade to him. I was grateful that he'd cheered Grandpa up so much, but we couldn't stand there talking all day. The Tomato-Matic 2000 was waiting.

Dominic set the plane down gently on the kitchen table, and I pushed the sliding door to the backyard open, motioning for him to step through first.

I was busy setting my lemonade down on the railing and sliding the screen door shut, when I heard Dominic call out cheerfully, "Hello there!"

I looked around to see who he was talking to, and there was our favorite neighbor, Mr. Petrecelli, trespassing on Grandpa's lawn *again*. He was standing near Tomato's cross, where I'd found him before, holding a pair of garden clippers, even though he wasn't clipping anything. I could tell from the look on his face that Dominic had startled him.

"No need to shout!" Mr. Petrecelli barked. "I can see you there."

"Oh. Sorry," Dominic said, using a much softer voice. He shouldn't have bothered. But then, he'd never met Mr. Petrecelli before. He didn't know yet that, no matter what he did, it would get on the old man's nerves.

"What's that?" Mr. Petrecelli said now. "I can't make out your mumbling."

I sighed and grabbed Dominic's arm. "Don't worry about him," I whispered. "That's my grandpa's neighbor. He's *always* like that."

"I heard that," Mr. Petrecelli announced, using an even angrier tone. "I wouldn't have to snap at you if you'd just leave me alone. Most people just want to be left alone, you know." He shuffled his feet in the grass. "I can't get a moment's peace back here with you kids running around shouting at the top of your lungs." He glanced at Tomato's cross again, then seemed to remember the clippers he was holding in his hand. "Aaaach," he grumbled. Then he hacked a single branch off a bush, as if that were what he'd come over for all along. "It's overgrown back here," he said. "Tell your grandfather to prune his bushes once in a while." He bent over stiffly to pick up the branch, then retreated into his own yard.

"Wow. What's with him?" Dominic said once he was gone.

"Trust me," I said. "I have *no* idea."

"Seems kind of lonely or something," Dominic offered.

I didn't know about that. Considering how much he hated people, you'd think being on his own would be exactly what Mr. Petrecelli wanted. Plus, he'd just told us to leave him alone.

"Seems kind of miserable if you ask me," I answered.

"Yeah," Dominic agreed. "But a lot of times there's more to people than they let you see."

I'd known Mr. Petrecelli my whole life, and if there was more to see, I hadn't seen it yet. It didn't seem worth arguing with Dominic, though. We had a ton of work in the backyard shed ahead of us. Before long Dominic was bound to see for himself what an old grump Mr. Petrecelli was.

"In here," I said, leading the way. I swung the latch on the door open and flicked on the light. "There it is!" I picked up the test newspaper I had sitting on the windowsill and tossed it onto the left side of the teeter-totter. The chain reaction began.

"The weight of the newspaper tips the teeter totter . . . ," Dominic said.

"Which tugs on the rope that releases the bowling ball . . . ," I went on, as we watched it happen.

"That falls onto the other side of the teeter-totter . . . "

WAP! The bowling ball landed with a thud in the big ice cream container I'd nailed to the teeter-totter to hold the ball in place.

"And catapults the newspaper into the air . . ." Dominic laughed as the weight of the bowling ball sent the *Somerville Times* flying in a perfect arc. "And it lands it right in the basket."

"Which starts off down the clothesline and travels in that direction," I said. "Until it gets stuck right there." I sighed. "Unless you raise the clothesline, and then it goes way too fast. My dad says we should put in a motor."

"That's a great idea," Dominic said. "Could we use that?" he pointed out an old tire swing that was gathering dust near the paint cans in the corner of the shed. I didn't know how an old tire swing was going to help us, but I was more than curious to find out. "Do you have a screwdriver?" he asked.

We detached the tire from the chains and took off the

swivel joint at the top, then rolled the tire back into the corner. What we really needed, Dominic explained, were the S-hooks and eyebolts. An hour later, using the metal parts we'd borrowed from the tire swing, along with a D cell battery and some alligator cable clips Dominic had in his backpack, we had a small, working motor. It coiled up a string that tugged on the clothesline, and *presto*—the basket holding the newspaper (which was held firmly by some of the S-hooks instead of the constantly breaking shoelaces I'd been trying to use) sailed smoothly to the end of the clothesline. I couldn't help it. I broke into applause, and Dominic gave a little bow, then brushed his hair back out of his eyes, grinning. "You already had most of it worked out," he said generously.

"Now we just need to figure out how to dump the newspaper and trigger the helicopter to make it lift the slippers," I said.

So we went back to the drawing board—literally. We hauled out a huge board that Grandpa had tucked behind his lawn mower, spread a bunch of paper on top of it, and started to sketch the machine using my smelly markers. I made the pulley system smell like cinnamon, then drew the newspaper in using the black licorice marker. At the top of the clothesline, I added a balloon, bright red and smelling like cherries. It looked pretty, and I had a feeling Rube Goldberg would have approved. "After all," I told Dominic, "drawing is what made Rube Goldberg really famous. He was a cartoonist."

"I didn't even know he was a real person," Dominic said, taking a break from adding green and purple stripes to the teeter-totter. He listened intently while I told him pretty much everything I knew about Rube Goldberg—which, thanks to Grandpa, was kind of a lot.

"The name of his most famous cartoon character was Professor Lucifer Gorgonzola Butts," I told Dominic, which made him burst out laughing. "He also wrote the script for the first movie the Three Stooges were in," I added.

"No way! My granddad used to show me their movies. They're those three guys who do stupid things, like smacking each other in the forehead and tripping each other, right?"

"Curly, Larry, and Moe," I said. When I was little, I'd named my three goldfish after them. Not that my goldfish ever slapped each other. Grandpa used to show me those movies too. They were so funny.

"My brothers and I used to play Three Stooges," Dominic said. "I was always Moe. One time we were playing at the Grand Canyon when we were on vacation, and my brother Ian tripped me, and I almost fell right in! I was only about five feet from the edge. I told on him, and he had to have a time-out in the car . . . so he missed the mule ride. He's still mad at me for that."

"I loved the mule ride!" I said. "The time we went, my mule was called Salty."

"Mine was Willow. Too bad they didn't name one Professor Lucifer Gorgonzola Butts," Dominic said, and then we both broke out laughing again. "Okay, how about this?" Dominic said when we'd finally gotten ourselves under control. He drew what looked like a small sword over the top of the balloon. "We can use a letter opener to pop the balloon from above. We'll need to trigger it somehow, of course."

He looked deep in thought, and while he started sketching out some possible mechanisms, I studied him carefully. I couldn't help thinking about what Dominic had said in the yard about Mr. Petrecelli. *A lot of times there's more to people than they let you see.*

Was it possible that was true about Dominic as well? Ever since he'd started stealing my science project ideas, I hadn't been able to look at him without thinking what a sneaky, underhanded copycat he was . . . but the Dominic I saw this day was different. He was funny. And smart. And kind of nice, even.

"Gorgonzola Butt," he muttered under his breath, and then laughed softly. "I'm going to use that one on my brother next time he calls me Nerd Face."

I smiled. It *was* a pretty funny name. I made a mental note to remember it. It might come in handy the next time Sarah took all the pepperonis on pizza night.

"Wait a sec!" he exclaimed. "Forget the balloon. I just thought of something better." I peered over his shoulder while he started to sketch. Then I grinned when I saw what he had planned.

"I like it," I said. "I like it a lot." And despite the small nervous feeling I still had in my stomach, I had to admit, I was actually starting to like Dominic, too. How weird was *that*?!

Chapter 7

A whole week had gone by, and with every passing day the science fair was getting closer, and the machine was getting bigger and better—but there was a long way to go yet. So even though we'd been putting it off for a while and that Friday was supposed to be the day Penny and I finally broke the tie in our backyard croquet match with Grandpa, I just couldn't fit it in.

Plus, Grandpa seemed so out of it that I was sure he'd forgotten all about our tournament anyway. The day before, when Dominic and I had arrived, we'd found him sitting in his armchair, staring at an old picture of him and Tomato on the beach. He'd looked a million miles away, and he hadn't even remembered to get up to offer us a snack.

"I'm really sorry," I told Penny as Dominic and I said good-bye to her outside the school. We were so close to perfecting the newspaper dump part of the Tomato-Matic 2000, and then we could move on to the slippers lift. I knew Penny would understand. "We'll finish the tournament soon, okay?" The science fair was just days away. It made my heart race to think about it.

"Sure," she said. "No problem. I'll see you tomorrow afternoon, though, right?"

"Definitely!" I answered, not wanting to hurt her feelings, even though I wasn't 100 percent sure I'd have time to hang out. I hadn't spent an afternoon with Penny in more than a week, and I wanted to see her, but it would kind of depend on how well the machine was working by then.

On our way to Grandpa's house, Dominic and I stopped by the hardware store again for a few supplies. Then we hit the fruit and veggie stand on the corner for one more thing. "You sure you want to use my idea?" Dominic said as we loaded ripe tomatoes into a bag. It was true that Dominic's suggestion for triggering the helicopter might get messy, but it was also pretty funny. Plus, there was the fact that Grandpa grew huge tomatoes every summer, and made his own sauce. Tomato had loved to eat grandpa's tomatoes too. It was how he'd gotten his name as a puppy. Really, Dominic's idea was meant to be.

"I'm sure," I said.

It took us most of that afternoon to rig up the catch at

the top of the clothesline that released when the newspaper basket hit it, then dumped the newspaper onto the coffee table and started a tomato rolling down a ramp.

On Saturday morning we both got to Grandpa's early and moved on to setting up the mannequin arm, which we'd found in the garbage outside a store. When the tomato reached the halfway mark on the ramp, it hit a lever that released a band we'd tied around the arm, dropping it just in time so that the mannequin hand smacked the tomato, turning it to juice that oozed into a bucket we'd set up underneath. The bucket was already filled with other smushed tomatoes, and the weight of the extra juice had to make it just heavy enough that it would fall off the ropes that were holding it and land on top of the helicopter liftoff button we'd placed underneath.

Dominic was programming the helicopter so that when the bucket hit the button, the helicopter would lift off the launchpad with the slippers attached and deliver them to the coffee table, where Grandpa would be waiting! TA-DA!

Of course, there were a few glitches to work out . . . including the fact that, when the bucket of juice fell onto the helicopter button, it kept tipping sideways and pouring squashed tomatoes all over the floor of the shed. Dominic and I had to work all afternoon to get it to stay steady.

"You ready?" Dominic asked finally as he tightened one last screw on the motor. We'd made a brace kind of thing with bent coat hangers, and it seemed to be holding the tomato bucket upright. There were still a bunch of other problems left to fix—the newspaper didn't always land in the basket when it flew off the catapult, and sometimes the motor stalled—but we'd come a long way, and it was time for a real test run. Of course I was ready! I couldn't wait to show the Tomato-Matic to Grandpa and see the grateful expression on his face when he realized that soon he wouldn't have to worry about bringing in the paper or finding his slippers anymore.

"Definitely." I smiled.

Minutes later Dominic and I were each tugging on one of Grandpa's hands, pulling him across the backyard. "Close your eyes, Grandpa," I said when we reached the shed door. We helped him across the threshold. "Okay. Open!" Grandpa grinned as he looked around the shed.

"I barely recognize the place!" He laughed. It was true. All of the paint cans and old boxes had been pushed to one side to make room for the Rube Goldberg machine. With the clothesline pulley system and tomato ramp stretched out, our machine went from wall to wall. It looked pretty impressive. We'd even borrowed some old Christmas lights and strung them up around the sign we'd painted in ruby-red one-foot-high letters. INTRODUCING THE TOMATO-MATIC 2000!

"Here." I handed Grandpa a rolled up newspaper. "I think you should do the honors. Toss that onto the left side of the teeter-totter, okay?" He did, and the Tomato-Matic went to work.

"It's for you," I explained as the teeter-totter tipped, pulling the string that released the bowling ball. It thudded onto the other side of the plank of wood and launched the paper directly into the wicker basket. Then Dominic's motor whirred to life, thankfully, without a hitch.

"When the science fair is over, I'm going to set it up in your house," I told Grandpa. "Then every morning when the paperboy comes, he'll throw the paper onto the plank, which we'll set up at the front door, and this is what will happen." By now the newspaper basket had reached the end of the pulley system. It hit the bumper pad, which released the catch and tapped the waiting tomato, which started its descent down the ramp. At the same time, the basket tipped and the newspaper fell squarely onto the coffee table that waited below.

"Would you look at that!" Grandpa said, obviously impressed.

The tomato reached the middle of the ramp and hit the lever that released the mannequin arm. *WAP!* The disembodied hand smacked the tomato to oblivion, sending seeds and juice flying everywhere. "That part is a bit messy," I explained.

Grandpa watched with fascination as the juice dripped down the ramp, filling the bucket and stretching the ropes to their breaking point. *BAM!* The bucket landed on top of the sensor that turned on the helicopter. But without warning the brace we'd built with bent coat hangers gave out, sending the bucket tipping sideways and releasing a sea of mashed tomato across the floor.

"Oh, no!" Dominic said. We'd been almost positive that we'd finally worked that bug out. "That's not supposed to happen," he said apologetically.

Still, the helicopter rose off its launchpad into the air, circling in a perfect arc, before setting the slippers down gently beside the coffee table.

Grandpa laughed and shook his head. "Now, that's one way of making tomato juice I've never seen before," he said. And that was when I realized he'd kind of missed the point. I mean, yes, the machine made tomato juice, but that wasn't its *real* job.

"See the slippers and newspaper," I pointed out. "It does the things Tomato used to do for you. That's why it's called the Tomato-Matic. It's like your new best friend! The tomato squishing part was just extra. That was Dominic's idea."

All of a sudden Grandpa seemed to stiffen. He cleared his throat. Then he got kind of quiet.

"Do you like it?" I asked, almost jumping up and down. Except for the tomatoes spilling, it had been one of the best runs the machine had ever had, and I was so proud Grandpa had been there to see it.

Instead of answering, Grandpa walked over to the machine, picked up the newspaper, and stared at the front page.

"Obviously that's an old paper. We just used it for the test. When we set it up for real, it'll be the one from that morning."

"I see. So this is my new dog, is it?" Grandpa said finally. He put down the paper, walked over to the tomato bucket, and set it upright. "Messier than the old one."

I thought he was making a joke, so I laughed. "Don't worry, Grandpa. We'll fix that part somehow."

"That's not what I'm worried about," he said, looking up at me now. His mouth was a tight, straight line. It wasn't an expression I saw often on Grandpa's face. "It's the rest of it that worries me." He took a step back to look at the entire machine. "Ruby, how would you feel if someone tried to replace Penny with cables and ramps?" Grandpa asked.

It was a crazy question. Of course a machine could never replace Penny!

"Penny isn't a dog," I said, pointing out the obvious.

"Tomato wasn't just a dog either. He was my best friend for thirteen long years. He was a lot more to me than a newspaper and slippers fetcher."

"I know that, Grandpa. I didn't mean that it's like a real dog, but the machine can help you. Doesn't it make you feel a little bit better?"

"No, Ruby," he snapped. "It doesn't. It makes me feel worse, if you want to know the truth. You know I adore you, but every now and then I wish you knew when to call it quits."

Grandpa's words hit me harder than a newspaper-filled basket to the head. When everyone else was telling me to stop showing off, stop taking their stuff for science experiments, stop making everything a contest, he'd always been the one encouraging me to explore new things and try a little bit harder to reach my goals. But now I knew the truth. He thought I took things too far too, just like my parents, and the kids at school, and everyone else except Penny.

"The Tomato-Matic," Grandpa said, and sighed, looking at our lit-up sign. "I'll tell you one thing. This might be an impressive piece of machinery, but I liked my old dog better."

I felt my eyes start to sting, and I knew the tears wouldn't be far behind. I picked up my backpack and ran out the shed door.

"Wait, Ruby!" It was Dominic, coming down the driveway toward me. "Are you okay?" I wiped furiously at my eyes with the back of my hand, trying to blot the tears that were trickling down my face now.

"Sure." I said, swinging one leg over my bike. "I'm fine. I just have to go home now, that's all."

"Oh," Dominic said, putting his backpack on. "Okay. Yeah. Me too." He took a few steps toward the street, but then stopped and turned around. "Are you sad because your grandpa didn't like it?" he asked, blinking from underneath his bangs.

"It's fine," I said, not wanting him to see how upset I was. Everyone already thought I was too competitive and too much of a show-off. The last thing I needed to hear was that I was too sensitive as well.

"Okay," Dominic said. "But if you were—sad, I mean—I'd

understand. I still think it's a great machine. And I bet your grandpa does too. He probably didn't mean what he said."

I kind of doubted that. Grandpa was such a careful, thoughtful, kind person. He wouldn't have said it if it weren't true. That was what made it hurt most of all. Still, it was nice of Dominic to try to make me feel better.

"Sure." I said, even though I didn't believe it. "Yeah. Maybe."

I took the long way home, circling through the park and then using the trail that ran along the river, but I was careful to leave myself enough daylight to get home safely.

The streetlights were just coming on as I reached my house, which was probably why I didn't notice Penny until I was partway up our front path—even though she should have been extremely noticeable. After all, it's not every day you come home to find a peacock sitting on your steps. Her skirt was bright yellow with green and blue eye shapes painted on it. Rows of colorful sequins ran around the bottom. She was also wearing a feathered headband and had thick green lines painted around her eyes. I could see that she was twirling her hair around one finger, that way she always does when she's nervous or upset.

"Penny!" I exclaimed, coming to a stop in front of her. "Your costume is so beautiful."

"Is it?" she said, raising her arms. Her peacock skirt glittered in the streetlights. "I didn't think you'd notice." And that was when I saw that the green face paint around her eyes was smudged, like she'd been crying.

I got off my bike, dumped it on the lawn, and went to sit beside her.

"Are you okay?" I asked.

She sniffed. "I was wondering the same thing about you when you didn't show up at my dress rehearsal. That's why I came straight here after, to see if you were all right . . . but your mom said you were still at your grandpa's."

The dress rehearsal! It had been that afternoon, and I'd promised to be right in the front row, where Penny could see me. That's what she'd meant on Friday when she'd said she'd see me the next day! I couldn't believe I'd completely forgotten!

"I'm so sorry," I said. Penny's face softened. "I should have remembered. It's just that Dominic and I were so close to finishing the Tomato-Matic 2000. It wasn't looking so good for a while, but today we finally found a way to steady the bucket of tomato juice when it lands on the helicopter trigger. We realized that if we built a brace out of bent coat hangers—except it didn't exactly work. Plus, you won't believe what my Grandpa said to me—"

"AGGHhhh!" Penny got up off the step and put her hands on her hips. Her skirt flared out around her in the breeze as she faced me. "Really?" she said. "You're talking about coat hangers right now?"

"What?" I answered helplessly. "What's wrong with coat hangers?"

"Nothing! It's just that lately all you talk about is Tomato-Matic this and Tomato-Matic that."

"But," I said, my voice small, "I thought you wanted to know about it."

"*Of course* I do," she said. "But it would be nice if you cared about my life sometimes too. You *promised* you'd be at the dress rehearsal."

"I know," I said meekly. "But I just forgot. I mean, there are so many details to remember for the science fair, and I—"

"Best friends don't forget," Penny said. "No matter what else is going on. I always do my best to help you, and you couldn't even remember to do this one thing for me!"

"Penny! I—"

But she didn't let me finish. She turned, her feathers swaying in the wind, and strutted up the path with her head held high, not looking back even once.

At first I wasn't worried. Penny hardly ever got mad at me, and she never stayed that way. Even the time when I threw her favorite fairy doll off the playhouse in first grade to make it fly, she hadn't held it against me for long. She just got her dad to superglue the head back on and forgave me later that afternoon.

But when I tried to call her after dinner, I started to see that this was much more serious than a beheaded fairy. She refused to even come to the phone.

"Maybe she just needs some time to cool down," Dominic

suggested when we met early the next morning at my grandpa's house.

"Maybe," I said, but I wasn't so sure. Dominic was a genius when it came to electronics (I couldn't believe how perfectly he'd programmed the helicopter to always land in the right spot with the slippers), but he clearly didn't know very much about girls. I'd hurt Penny's feelings badly, and if I wanted to make it up to her, giving her time to cool down wasn't going to cut it. I was going to have to do something big . . . something to show her how truly, honestly sorry I was. I just wasn't sure what yet. Then I also had the problem of Grandpa to worry about. When we got to his place, he acted like he was busy cleaning out a closet that was filled with some of Tomato's old leashes and toys, and he barely said anything to me—so I knew that Dominic had been wrong. Grandpa really *had* meant what he'd said. Just like Ms. Slate and all the kids at school, he thought I was obsessed with winning and never knew when to stop. And with Penny mad at me, as sad as that was, now the only person I had on my side at all was Dominic.

"What if we twisted the coat hangers around something really heavy to form a solid base?" Dominic suggested. "Then the bucket wouldn't be able to tip." We were standing in the shed, trying to fix the machine's last and messiest problem. "Like these," he said, picking up some bricks that were stacked next to the lawn mower.

It seemed like a decent idea, so we got started, untwisting

the ends of the coat hangers with pliers, then re-twisting them through the holes in the bricks. But it was slow, boring, and frustrating work. The coat hangers were stiff, and the pointy ends kept springing loose from the pliers and scratching my arm.

"Aaaargh!" I shouted when I lost my grip on the hanger for about the millionth time. "I hate this!"

"It *is* a little tricky," Dominic said calmly. "You'll get better control if you hold the pliers closer to the end of the wire."

"That's not what I meant," I said, giving the Tomato-Matic a dirty look. "I mean I hate this whole machine. I wish we'd never built it!" After all, it had ruined everything. Not only had the Tomato-Matic hurt Grandpa's feelings and made him mad at me, but it had caused me to have a fight with Penny, too. If the science fair hadn't been just a day away, I would have kicked the machine.

"You hate our project?" Dominic said.

What? Had I not said it loudly enough? "Yes. I do!" Dominic didn't answer. He just stared at me, looking baffled. Then he blinked in that infuriating way he had. The he blinked *again*. Then *again*! Suddenly I couldn't stand it a second longer.

"Stop blinking at me!" I yelled.

"What do you mean?" he asked.

"I mean exactly what I said," I answered. "Stop opening and closing your eyes. It's annoying." I tried to go back to untwisting my coat hanger, but I lost my grip on it again and it sprung loose, digging into my arm. This time my arm actually started to bleed a little. "Oh, forget it!" I said, throwing down my pliers. "I can't stand this anymore. You finish it!"

"Okay," Dominic said softly. He was holding his eyes wide open in this ridiculous way now. Instantly I felt terrible. Dominic was trying so hard to help me. He was the last person I should have been mad at. Actually, the only person I should have been the least bit angry with was myself. If I'd been a little more considerate of the people who were always on my side, I could have prevented all these problems in the first place.

"I'm sorry, Dominic," I said. "I didn't really mean any of that. You can blink all you want to. It's probably good for your eyes, I bet. I should do it more myself." I blinked my eyes about ten times in a row to show him how much I meant it.

"It's okay," he said gently. "I know you're just frustrated. I'll finish the coat hangers. Go home and take a break or something. You did the whole first part of the machine on your own anyway, so I owe you."

There he was again, saying he owed me when really he didn't. I could see that now. He was a nice person—and if he'd copied my projects before, it wasn't to steal the gold medal from me. After all, scientists were always copying one another, and then building on to one another's discoveries. It was how they made progress and learned new things.

"Thanks, Dominic," I said. "You're a good friend." I could

hardly believe those words were coming out of my mouth, but they were true. "I probably *should* go take a break. I'll see you tomorrow, okay?"

I pedaled my bike home furiously, letting the wind whip through my hair. I rode twice around the block, then took a detour through the park, trying to clear my head. Two girls my age were on the swing set, laughing their heads off as they swung high enough to almost flip over the bar. I knew one of them from summer camp, so I smiled at her, but she was too busy giggling to notice. I kept pedaling past an older couple bent over near the jungle gym, where they were trying (and failing) to keep a baby from eating big handfuls of sand. Then I whizzed past a man who was throwing a ball for his dog. It was a blue one with red stripes, just like the one Grandpa used to throw for Tomato. I pedaled faster, eager to leave the park behind now. All the happy friends, caring grandparents, and ball-chasing dogs there only made me feel sadder about everything that was going on.

When I got home, I parked my bike around back and went into the kitchen. Getting mad always makes me hungry, and I was craving crackers and cheese. I found my sister in the kitchen, where, as usual, she was doing the same thing I wanted to do—only better. She'd arranged Melba Toasts on a plate and topped them with slices of Swiss cheese and fresh herbs, and was just popping her plate into the microwave.

"Cheese and crackers show-off," I muttered under my breath as I went to get the Kraft Singles and soda crackers.

"Well, hello to you, too," Sarah said sarcastically, putting a basil leaf into her mouth and chewing it. "What's wrong? Trouble in science-fair-land?" She plopped down on a chair and hugged her knees to her chest.

"No," I said. "We're almost finished with the machine."

"Well, good!" she answered. "So now you'll finally stop stealing my stuff?"

I couldn't stand it anymore. It was bad enough that Penny and Grandpa were mad at me—and that I'd been so mean to Dominic, who didn't deserve it one bit. I knew I was a bad friend, and a bad granddaughter . . . but now I had to hear about how I was a bad sister, too? "I'm sorry!" I shouted. "Just leave me alone, okay?"

Sarah held up her hands like she was stopping traffic. "Okay, okay," she said. "Sheesh. I know you already promised. And you gave my shoelaces back. I was just kidding, okay?"

The microwave beeped, and I pulled it open and handed Sarah her plate. Her snack looked amazing and smelled even better. I replaced it with my plate of plain soda crackers and processed cheese, then slammed the microwave door shut and hit the thirty-seconds button.

"Here," Sarah said, handing me a Melba Toast. I sat down at the table and started to nibble miserably at one corner. It was depressingly delicious. "Seriously. What's wrong?" she asked.

"Nothing," I answered, looking down at the table.

"It's *not* nothing," she said reasonably.

"Okay, fine. It's Penny." I told Sarah about how I'd missed

the dress rehearsal for her peacock dance, and how she was mad at me because all I ever talked about was my Rube Goldberg machine. And once I'd started talking, I couldn't stop. I also told her about how disappointed in me Grandpa had been—and about how he thought I'd been trying to replace Tomato with a machine, and how I'd been mean to Dominic because I was just so frustrated. "But I didn't mean to ruin everything and make everyone mad!" I wailed. "I just wanted to help Grandpa. It's the only reason I took your shoelaces and your coat hangers too. I wanted to make the best machine possible. What's so wrong with that?"

By then the microwave had long since finished. I opened the door and grabbed my plate. My cheese slices had melted into a lake of orange grease, and the crackers were soggy. Great! I couldn't even make a snack right.

Sarah took one look at my cheese mess and handed me another Melba Toast.

"There's nothing wrong with wanting to make the best science fair project possible," she said, then chewed thoughtfully for a while. "You just need to remember that it's not the *most important* thing."

Easy for her to say! She was so good at everything that she never needed to worry. She could win the Rachel Halloway Lloyd Award for Excellence in Science, get an A on her English essay, and still find time to hang out at the mall with her friends, all while creating amazing snacks using foreign melted cheeses and fresh herbs.

"I mean, if you don't win the gold medal, who cares?"

I cared! I cared a lot! And, based on the huge fuss they'd made over Sarah's stupid science award, so did Mom and Dad.

"Penny definitely won't care. And neither will Grandpa," Sarah said. "They care more about you spending time with them . . . and taking an interest in *their* lives once in a while."

"I'm interested in their lives," I answered defensively.

"Are you?" Sarah asked, not unkindly. "What's Penny doing for her science project?"

"I . . . ummm." For the first time it occurred to me that I honestly didn't know.

"And have you ever asked her to show you part of the dance she's working on?"

"Well, no . . . but . . . she's *told* me about it."

"How about Grandpa? What has he been doing all day without Tomato these last few weeks?"

"Sleeping, I think."

Okay, so maybe Sarah had a point.

"Look at Rube Goldberg," she went on. Sarah had heard as many Rube Goldberg stories as I had growing up. Probably more, since she was older. "He designed amazing machines, but he was also a cartoonist, and an engineer, and an inventor. *And* he had kids *and* he was married. He gave lots of things and lots of people his attention."

I sighed. She was right, of course. I wanted to win the science fair so badly, but there were other things that mattered more. If I lost my best friend and hurt my grandfather's feelings along the way, was it worth it?

"Okay," I admitted. "I get it. But how do I make them forgive me?" Sarah had tons of friends. She was good at this stuff. "Maybe I could make Grandpa an album out of old photos of Tomato," I suggested. "And if I could find an old dog footprint someplace in the backyard, I could cast it in plaster of paris and mount it in a frame. And Penny likes dancing, right?" I went on, getting one idea after another. "Maybe I could get some kids together and do a big choreographed routine? We could surprise her in the school yard. It would have to be a song about how sorry I am, and I'd lip sync it to her. Do you know a good song? Can I borrow your iPod?"

Sarah smiled. "You know, Ruby, I think that might be part of your problem."

What? That I didn't have my own iPod?

"You don't always have to make simple things so complicated. Why not, for once, do something the easy way? Just say you're sorry."

"But I already tried calling Penny to say I was sorry!" I wailed. "She wouldn't even talk to me."

"Well, try again," Sarah said. She passed me the plate with the last Melba Toast on it. I took it, ate it, and then got up to scrape my plate of cheese goo into the organic waste bin.

Just say I'm sorry? I thought as I watched the goo plop into the bag. It sounded so easy. Too easy, almost. But maybe Sarah was right. Doing things the complicated way didn't seem to be getting me anywhere lately. And just saying I was sorry had worked with Dominic.

"Trust me, okay?" Sarah said. I did. "And if it still doesn't work, I'll help you with the dog book and the dance routine, okay?" she promised.

I grinned. Sarah was all right, I guessed. I was pretty lucky to have a sister like her.

For a second I started considering ways to show her how much I appreciated her advice—maybe by running upstairs to make her a pop-up thank you card or an "I will clean your room for one week" gift certificate out of construction paper with glitter glued around the edges—but then I thought better of it. "Thanks," I said simply.

Sarah smiled. "You're welcome."

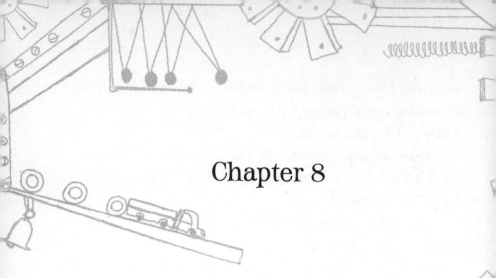

Chapter 8

But even though saying "I'm sorry" to Penny sounded simple, it was actually pretty complicated. First of all I had to track her down, and then I had to keep up with her.

It was later that day—mere hours before her big dance show—and if I thought the life of a scientist was demanding, well, turns out it's got *nothing* on the life of a dancer!

I rode my bike over to her place at three, but her dad said she wasn't home. "She and her mom went to pick up a few things," he explained when I knocked on the door. "She should be back in a little while, if you want to come in and wait. Unless . . ." He pulled some kind of schedule out of his back pocket and consulted it. "Wait. That's not right. She's got a hair appointment at three fifteen at Ingrid's Salon.

Apparently you need a professional to get the peacock head-band on just right." He smiled. "I'll tell her you stopped by, okay?"

"That's okay," I said. "Maybe I can catch her at the hair place."

So I rode my bike downtown and parked it outside the salon. The beauty shop was packed with peacocks—along with swarms of little girls with their faces painted to look like butterflies and bumblebees. It took me a while to find her, but I finally spotted Penny sitting in the reception area. She was holding her feathered headband in her lap, waiting her turn. I tapped on the glass to get her attention, and two butterflies ran over. One of them smushed her face up against the glass.

"Kimmy!" her mother shrieked, pulling her away. "You'll ruin your makeup." Sure enough, the girl left a big wing-print behind on the windowpane. While the mother led Kimmy back to a makeup chair, I tapped again. This time Penny turned her head and saw me, but looked away just as fast.

I wasn't about to give up that easily. I opened the door and stepped into the salon.

"Hi there." The receptionist gave me a glowing white smile. "Are you with the Downtown Dance Studio?" I shook my head, and her smile vanished. "Sorry," she said. "We're booked up right now. Big recital this tonight."

"But I just needed to—"

"Sorry," she said again, cutting me off. "Come back next week, or call to book an appointment, okay?"

"But could I just talk to—?"

She came around the desk, put a hand on my shoulder, and led me to the door. "Sorry, sweetheart," she said. "Another day, okay?"

I sighed and stepped out onto the street, discouraged but not defeated. If they wouldn't let me in, well, then, I'd just have to talk to Penny from outside. Thinking quickly, I ripped a garage sale notice off a telephone pole and flipped it over, then wrote in big block letters on the back using a stubby pencil I'd had in my pocket.

I went back to the window, held up my sign, and knocked again. This time a little bee buzzed over. She looked about four or five—too young to read.

"What does that say?" she asked.

"It says 'Sorry, Penny!'" I shouted.

The little girl shrugged like she couldn't hear me. "Tell Penny I'm sorry, okay?" I said, mouthing the words clearly, so she'd get it. "Penny!" I shouted, then pointed to where Penny was sitting.

"Okay," the little bee said, and skipped off. But if Penny ever got the message, she didn't seem to care. A minute later she got up and went for her turn in the hairdresser's chair, not even glancing in my direction.

So I waited. . . . First I practiced standing on one foot. Next I named the pigeons that were sitting on the roof of the grocery store across the street—which was a lot harder than it sounds. They kept moving, making it practically impossible to remember which one was Bob, which one was Maurice, and which one was Raphael. After I gave up on pigeon naming, I started picking litter up off the sidewalk to be a good citizen. I found a coffee cup, some rusted paperclips, and a plastic streamer, and I was just about finished rigging them up to make a working elevator for the ants in one of the flower boxes, when Penny's mom came out to see what I was doing.

"Ruby!" she said, sticking her head out the door. "Would you like to come in and sit down with us?"

I looked over her shoulder into the hair salon and saw Penny scowling at me from the hairdresser's chair.

"I don't think so, Mrs. Parker," I answered. "The receptionist already said I can't go in. Plus, Penny probably wouldn't like it. She's pretty mad at me."

"Hmmm. I heard something about that. Don't worry," she whispered. "I think she'll come around." She was holding a cookie tin in her hand, and when she saw me notice it, she held it out to me. "These are for the dancers," she explained, "but would you like one?"

They were granola snacks—kind of like the ones Penny had given me to taste test before, except not as crumbly. Since I hadn't had an afternoon snack yet, I *was* pretty starving.

"To keep your strength up!" Penny's mom said, smiling at me as I took one. "Don't give up, okay?" She winked at me, then disappeared back into the salon.

So I sat on the edge of a planter box and ate, sharing a few crumbs with Bob, Maurice, Raphael, and the ants. And when I was done, my strength was definitely renewed.

A half hour later Penny came out of the salon in full peacock hair and makeup. I hid behind a bush until her mom's car pulled away from the curb. Then I followed on my bike.

Instead of driving home, they went halfway across town to pick up Penny's little cousin. Then they stopped at the dance store, where Penny's mom bought her a new pair of ballet slippers. I parked my bike out front and went in, pretending to be browsing for leotards.

"Psst! Penny!" I whispered, peering through a spinning rack of sparkle tights.

She looked up.

"I'm sorry!" I whispered.

She half smiled, and for a second I thought that meant she was about to forgive me, but then she tapped her cousin's shoulder to get his attention. *Come,* she signed to him, and they went off to find her mom at the cash register.

Next they stopped at Fabric City to get some yellow thread. Then it was back to Penny's place for a final costume adjustment. I was exhausted from so much pedaling and groveling, but I was *not* going to give up.

The show was starting at seven, and I didn't want to disturb Penny, so I stopped home for dinner, then got back onto my bike and headed over to the concert hall to wait. I spent the next half hour on the lawn in front of the auditorium, picking every dandelion I could find—and there were plenty! Still, I was first in line when they opened the door, which meant I got the best seat in the house. Front row, center.

The little bees danced first—well, most of them. Two just stood in the center of the stage holding hands, looking shocked by all the lights and people. The butterflies were up next with a number where they flapped and pirouetted around the stage to classical music. The little kids were cute, of course, but the real professionals were the peacocks. You could tell by the hush that came over the room when they stepped onto the stage. Their costumes were so beautiful, and Penny—the lead peacock—was the most stunning of all.

I waved my arms wildly to get her attention, which made the people behind me grumble about how I was ruining their video recording, but I didn't care. For a split second before the music began, Penny looked right at me.

Sorry, I signed, by making a sign language *S* and moving it across my chest. Then I held up one hand and karate chopped it with the other from underneath and touched the base of one palm with the side of my other hand. *Kick bottom,* I mouthed.

Penny's face broke into a wide smile, and I didn't think it was just for the audience. Or at least I hoped it wasn't. And I knew it for sure after the show when she came to find me in the lobby.

"These are for you," I said, handing her the football-size bouquet of dandelions I'd picked while waiting outside the concert hall. "You did an amazing job! When you did those peacock hands . . ." I tried to do it, but even when I was making my best effort, I *still* looked more like a drowning chicken. "It seemed so real! And I loved the part where the other peacocks were waving the feathers around you."

"Thanks," she said, almost shyly. Then she added, "I'm glad you came."

"I'm glad I did too," I answered. "And I'm *sorry* about missing the dress rehearsal yesterday."

"I know," she said. "You sort of mentioned that a few times today, in a few different ways." She laughed, and then she brought me over to meet her dance teacher, Miss Leung. And just like that everything was back to normal.

Just say you're sorry, I thought to myself, as I biked home from the recital. So it really could be that easy. I just hoped it would work for Grandpa, too.

And you know what? It turns out it *did* work! What's more . . . you could even apologize over the phone! Because I had a ton of homework the next day, I decided to call Grandpa after school instead of going over. I said the words the second he picked up.

"I'm sorry."

"Ruby?" Grandpa said.

"Yeah. It's me. Ruby," I told him. "I'm calling to apologize."

"I'd gathered that last part," he said.

"I never meant for my science project to replace Tomato. I just wanted to cheer you up. And help you with your slippers and newspaper."

Grandpa sighed a little. "I'm sorry too," he said. "I overreacted when you showed me your Rube Goldberg machine, and I've been ashamed of myself ever since. I've just been sad. And a little lonely. But I shouldn't have taken it out on you." He cleared his throat, like he was embarrassed. "As much as I appreciate your efforts, I think it's time I started to get my own paper, don't you? And I haven't been on a walk since Tomato died. It's probably time I got back out into the world. In any case," he went on, "I assume you'll be coming by after supper to pick up this impressive piece of machinery. The science fair opens tomorrow, if I remember right. You'll need to get this giant contraption to the gym so they can award you and Dominic your gold medal on Wednesday night."

It made me smile to think that grandpa believed in my project so much, and I hoped he was right about the gold medal. But at the same time the Tomato-Matic didn't feel quite as important anymore. After all, a really good science project shouldn't just be an impressive chemical reaction or a series of observations. It should improve people's lives somehow. The whole point of the project had been to make Grandpa feel better about losing Tomato, and that hadn't exactly worked out.

Of course, I didn't realize until later that night that—in the roundabout way Rube Goldberg machines have—the Tomato-Matic 2000 was about to help me help Grandpa in a way I never could have expected.

When we got to Grandpa's house that evening, my dad stayed in to help him change a few lightbulbs, and I went straight to the shed. Dominic had finished making the coat hanger and bricks brace, just like he'd promised. It looked pretty solid. I went back to the car to get some of the collapsed boxes we'd brought for packing the machine, and I was carrying such a big stack of them to the shed that I could hardly see where I was going.

"You again?" Mr. Petrecelli said, making me jump.

"Hi, Mr. Petrecelli." I put the boxes down on the grass. With all the hurt feelings and misunderstandings I'd just sorted out, I really wasn't in the mood to have any more fights that day, so instead I tried an entirely new approach. "How are you tonight?" I asked in my most pleasant, least insolent voice.

"How do you think I am?" he snapped. "With this unseasonable heat we've been having!"

"Hot, probably." It seemed like a safe guess. We stood there in silence. "That cross is for Tomato," I said after a while. "In case you were wondering. That's my grandpa's dog that died. Grandpa called him Tomato because he used to love to eat tomatoes from the backyard. He also loved to chase croquet balls . . . and lick crumbs off the floor. Grandpa hardly ever needed to vacuum."

I was expecting Mr. Petrecelli to mutter something then about how much Tomato had also liked to pee on his poppies, but instead he looked down at the cross and said, "I lost my cat, Firenze, a little over a year ago. She died of cancer. She liked tomatoes too. Very unusual for a cat." He was quiet for a minute, and just when I thought he was about to turn and go, he went on. "We named her after the city we honeymooned in. Firenze, Italy. She was my wife's cat, really. She was never quite the same after Margaret died. I think she never stopped missing her mother."

Mr. Petrecelli had had a wife? She must have died a long time ago. I couldn't remember anyone else ever living with him. Although, now that I thought about it, there did used to be an old cat that slept on his porch. A brown tabby with black ear tips. Sometimes Tomato used to bark at it, but I hadn't seen it around in a long, long time.

"I'm sorry your cat died," I said.

"So am I," the old man answered. "And I'm sorry about your dog. I left your grandfather a plant on his front porch. I don't suppose he ever brought it in. Gardening helped me when I lost Firenze."

So it had been Mr. Petrecelli who'd left the little houseplant for Grandpa—the one with the blue wrapping the same exact color as Tomato's collar! Maybe Dominic had been right. It was possible Mr. Petrecelli wasn't so horrible after all. He was just kind of sad, a lot like Grandpa had been lately. Suddenly I had an idea.

"You know," I said cautiously, "if you ever have time, maybe you and my grandpa could hang out together. You could start a dead pets club." The second the words had left my mouth, I knew how awful they sounded. "Or not," I added quickly. "But Grandpa was just saying that he should start going for walks again. Maybe you could go with him sometime."

"What? With my bad knee?" Mr. Petrecelli tapped his cane on the grass.

"Oh. Right. Well, you don't have to walk. Maybe you and Grandpa could sit on your front porch and kill some flies together."

I felt a little sorry for the flies, of course, but if it meant Grandpa would have someone to talk to . . .

"Hmm," Mr. Petrecelli said, examining a branch on Grandpa's hedge. "I haven't seen much of Alfred except in passing, out in the yard, since your grandmother died. She and Margaret used to be the best of friends. They were always sitting out here doing their crochet, yakking away."

I looked toward the patio where Mr. Petrecelli was pointing, and I tried to imagine my grandmother sitting there laughing with Mr. Petrecelli's wife, Firenze the cat curled at their feet. My grandmother had died before I was born, and Grandpa didn't talk about her very often. I think it made him

too sad. I only knew what she looked like from a picture he had up in the hall.

Mr. Petrecelli picked a tiny bug off a leaf and flicked it to the ground. "I suppose I could go walking. Not every day, mind you. But sometimes a walk in the morning is pleasant enough. Before the worst of this heat sets in. It gets the digestion going. I'll talk to your grandfather about it next time I see him."

I smiled, but because I wasn't sure exactly how much I wanted to know about Mr. Petrecelli's digestion, I was thankful when he changed the subject

"What is it you're doing back there with your boyfriend, anyway, making all that noise?" he asked.

"Dominic is *NOT* my boyfriend," I almost shouted, nearly shuddering at the thought.

It was the first time I'd ever seen Mr. Petrecelli actually smile.

"He's *just* my science fair partner. We're making a Rube Goldberg machine that fetches a paper and slippers."

"Ah!" he said. "Rube Goldberg. I used to enjoy his cartoons."

I raised my eyebrows. Who knew? Maybe Mr. Petrecelli and Grandpa were going to have even more in common than I thought.

"Well. Best of luck with that endeavor, I suppose," Mr. Petrecelli grumbled. Then he turned and walked back to his house, but this time he didn't slam the screen door behind him. I could hardly believe it. He was like a completely different person!

"And mind you keep off my flowers," he added, sticking his head back out.

Well, maybe not *completely* different . . . but it was progress, at least.

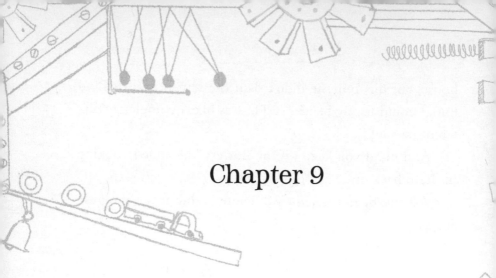

Chapter 9

On the first day of the science fair, the air is always thick with excitement, and the halls are always filled with weird stuff. Heather Greenbelt came in with some kind of enormous Ferris wheel with wires sticking out of it, Supeng and Eleni had a big poster board with pictures of bald people glued to it, and Mike Reynolds. was carrying an extremely stinky tray of what looked like rotting mangoes—except they were green and fuzzy, so it was hard to tell for sure.

"We'll head down to the gym to set up right after morning announcements," Ms. Slate said. She wrinkled her nose slightly. "Mike," she added, "maybe you can leave your decomposition-of-foods project in the hallway until then."

It took me and Dominic four trips from the classroom

to the gym to move the pieces of the Tomato-Matic 2000, and nearly all of first period to set it up—and that was with Penny helping us. Her project was just a simple display board, so luckily she had extra time. Otherwise we might still be working.

Even though we'd put a ton of thought into the different parts of our Rube Goldberg machine, one thing we hadn't remembered to think about was how, exactly, we were going to set it up someplace other than Grandpa's shed. It had been easy enough to bolt the clothesline into the wooden beams there, but we weren't allowed to drill into the school walls, and anyway, they were made of cement blocks. It took a lot of duct tape and some serious patience to get the job done. When we'd finally finished, we had only a few minutes left to walk around the gym to check out the competition.

There were the projects you'd expect, like a model solar system made of golf balls and wire, a demonstration on the oxidization of metals, and even a basic vinegar-and-baking-soda volcano or two . . . but even those were well done, with tidy graphs and neatly written observations.

"Nice job on the rings of Saturn," I said to Toby Jones. "What did you make them out of?"

"Different colors of telephone wire," he answered, eyeing me uncertainly.

"Great idea!" I said. "Hey. Cool pie chart!" I told Brianne. She'd obviously made it on the computer. It had a 3-D effect to it and looked awesome.

"Thanks," she said, giving me a strange look.

"Did Ruby just say 'nice job'?" I overheard Toby whispering to Brianne as I walked away from their projects.

"I know!" Brianne answered.

I smiled to myself. Maybe if I just kept following my sister's advice and paying attention to other people and their accomplishments, the kids in my class would eventually forgive me for the Hershey's Kisses incident . . . and the honey field trip fiasco . . . and all the other times I'd been a little less than considerate.

Dominic and I kept walking and checked out some of the *really* impressive projects on the other side of the gym, like Aaron Smith's study about how Egyptian mummies were made, complete with a semi-gross demonstration of the way they used to pull people's brains out through their noses. (He'd made it using a plastic baby doll with a hollow head, a ball of wool, and a crochet hook.) Then there was Peter's optical illusions display, where he was marking down whether boys or girls were better at seeing hidden shapes in different pictures. (So far, girls were winning by a landslide.) And there was Heather's solar-powered Ferris wheel.

"This is really cool," Dominic said when we came to Penny's project. She smiled shyly.

Her poster board said dance power at the top in rainbow bubble letters. Then there were lots of colorful graphs and photos of kids, with quotes written underneath. I recognized a few of the kids in the pictures as the bumblebees from the hair salon and dance recital. Underneath the title, Penny had written her investigation question: *Which snack foods give dancers the most long-lasting energy?* Sitting beside the poster board was a big cookie tin full of the same kind of granola snacks Penny's mom had given me at the hair salon. Penny passed us both the tin.

"Can I have one too?" Supeng asked, leaving her project to come over.

"These are so good!" said Samantha, taking a bite. "What's in them, Penny?"

Before long a small line of people had started to form. I took another bite. They were delicious, and I wanted to know what was in them too, but just then I heard a faint ripping sound, and Dominic and I both gasped and ran over to our project just in time to stop the pulley system from coming un-taped from the wall. We added half a roll of duct tape, which seemed to work for the moment, but clearly we were going to have to come up with a better solution . . . and we didn't have long to do it either. Parents' Night and the judging and awards ceremony were the next day!

Penny and Dominic both came to Grandpa's after school, and, using two old stepladders and a lot of rope, we managed to build a pretty solid stand for the pulley system. Dominic had a dentist appointment the next morning, but Penny came to school early to help me set it up, proving yet again that she's definitely the world's best best friend.

It was strange to be there on our own in the gym between the rows and rows of projects. "Who do you think is going to win?" I asked after we'd finished. We were walking up and down the aisles, getting one last look at the projects before the bell rang.

"Definitely you and Dominic," Penny said without hesitating. "I mean, look around! These projects are great, but who else built an entire machine, plus a working model helicopter? What you guys did is amazing." I hoped that the judges would agree, but more than anything, I was ready for it to be over. My stomach was so tied up in knots that I hadn't even been able to eat my cereal that morning. I didn't manage to eat much lunch, either. I also couldn't seem to sit still for dinner that night.

By the time my parents, my sister, Grandpa, and I got to the gym at six thirty for the judging and awards ceremony, I was so starving that even Mike's rotting mangoes were looking pretty good.

"Here," Penny said, handing me one of her granola bars. She'd had to bake a fresh batch the night before, and she was already running low. "Don't even go near those mangoes."

I took the granola bar gratefully.

"Ruby!" Dominic called, his voice squeaking in anticipation. "It's almost time!" The science fair judges were making notes on their clipboards as Aaron did his demonstration of the mummy brains. That meant we were up next.

"Looks like the big moment has finally arrived," Grandpa said as he joined us beside our project.

"I can't wait to see it!" my mom agreed.

"It *does* look pretty cool," Sarah admitted.

Kick bottom, Penny signed, grinning.

"And here we have Ruby Goldberg and Dominic Robinson's Rube Goldberg machine," Ms. Slate told the judges as she led them over. "Ruby, do you want to tell us a little bit about it?"

A small crowd had gathered, waiting to see the machine in action.

"Well," I said, clearing my throat. I'd been planning to talk about the gravitational forces that were at work, and how the levers and weights and motor propelled the machine, but suddenly something about the speech I'd planned felt wrong.

"Ruby?" Dominic said softly. And that was when I realized what it was. I mean, yeah, the science was impressive, but it wasn't the *most important* part.

"Sorry," I said. Then I gave the judges a smile. "This is the Tomato-Matic 2000. Like Ms. Slate said, it's a Rube Goldberg machine, which means that it uses a lot of steps to perform a simple task. And, trust me, it was a real team effort. Not only did my family and my best friend help me," I said, "but Dominic and I combined the usual forces at work in a Rube Goldberg machine—like gravity and friction—with electronics, which is Dominic's specialty. And that's what makes our project unique." I glanced over and saw that Dominic was beaming. "And now," I said, building up the suspense, "without further ado . . . Dominic will show you how it works."

Dominic looked at me in surprise. To tell the truth I was a little shocked myself. After all, the project had been my idea. I'd always pictured myself taking the spotlight when it was time to show the machine to the judges, but somehow it felt like the right thing to do. I handed him the rolled up newspaper and gave a little nod for him to go on.

"In essence," Dominic said, his voice shaking a bit, "the Tomato-Matic 2000 fetches the paper and gets your slippers, just like a pet dog might do. It's dedicated to the memory of Ruby's grandpa's dog, whose name was Tomato . . . which is why the machine also harnesses the power of tomatoes to do its work."

Everyone laughed as he picked up a ripe tomato and set it at the top of the ramp to prepare the machine. I glanced over at Grandpa to see if he was upset about Dominic mentioning Tomato, but he was smiling along with everyone else, watching intently as Dominic threw the newspaper onto the teeter-totter and the machine came to life.

The crowd oohed as the wooden plank tipped, releasing the bowling ball into the ice cream container that launched the newspaper into the basket. They aahed as the motor whirred and carried the basket down the clothesline. Everyone smiled as the newspaper tipped out and landed on the coffee table. Then the tomato was released down the ramp. Some people laughed, and others jumped back in surprise (and to avoid getting splattered) when the mannequin hand wacked the ripe tomato. Then the bucket filled just enough and, *BOOM*, dropped, landing on the sensor, where the brace made from bricks and coat hangers held it steady. "Watch out!" Dominic warned as the tiny helicopter lifted off, carrying the slippers. When it deposited them right beside the chair we'd set up, everyone broke into applause.

"That was amazing, Ruby!" Sarah said.

"Great job, honey," Mom added, tucking a stray strand of hair behind my ear.

"That part with the arm and the tomato," Dad said, still laughing. "Genius!"

"Quite an accomplishment." Grandpa grinned. "You should be very proud of yourself." And you know what? I was. Dominic extended his hand, and I shook it. I was proud of both of us.

Even though I knew we'd done the best we could do, the next half hour, while we waited for the other projects to be judged, was still agony. The only thing that made it bearable was that my appetite seemed to have come back, and Penny had saved me the last of her granola snacks. Finally Ms. Slate climbed up onto the stage and tapped the microphone.

"Excuse me. Could I have your attention please?" A hush fell over the gym, and everyone turned to look at the stage. "Hello, friends and family, and welcome to the Scott

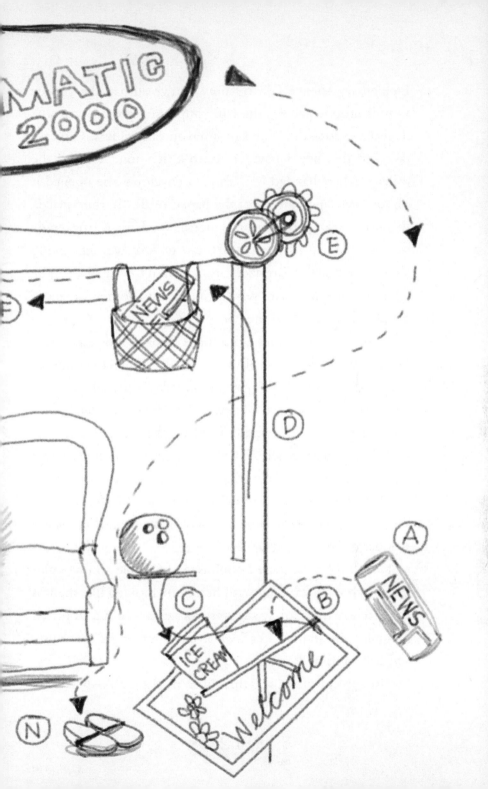

Elementary science fair. By now you've all had the chance to walk around and see the truly impressive projects our students have done this year. I'm sure you can tell it was no easy task, but the judges have come to a decision." One of the other teachers handed Ms. Slate an envelope. She opened it oh so slowly and pulled out the paper inside. "In third place," she read, "taking the bronze medal, we have a true engineering marvel." I felt my heart start to sink. Was she talking about our project? Bronze? Bronze wasn't even silver! Still, it was possible Ms. Slate was talking about another project—Heather's Ferris wheel, maybe.

"Ruby Goldberg and Dominic Robinson showed us how forces at work can be combined with electronics to complete a series of steps and perform simple tasks," she said.

Everyone applauded. I knew I was supposed to do something, but my feet seemed glued to the spot. "Come on, Ruby!" Dominic was tugging on my sleeve. I followed him up to accept our bronze medals, feeling like I was about to cry.

"Well done, Ruby. Well done, Dominic," Ms. Slate said as she put the medals around our necks. "Your machine was a wonder to behold."

From up on the stage I could see my whole family—plus Penny, who was standing with her mom, looking like she was about to cry too. I knew she was worried about me, so I tried to smile. She twirled her hair around her finger nervously and smiled back.

"In second place, for the silver medal . . ."—Ms. Slate

paused for dramatic effect—"is a young scientist who gathered quantitative data to solve a real-world problem in a tasty way. Penny Parker's Dance Power project showed us that snacks made from whole grains and natural substances like honey do a better job of giving dancers long-term energy than sugary snacks or energy drinks." Everyone started to applaud even louder now. Somebody put their fingers in their mouth and gave a shrill whistle, and Penny started up the steps to the stage, looking even more stunned than I felt. She came to stand beside me and Dominic, her mouth partly open.

"Congratulations, Penny!" Ms. Slate said as she put the silver medal around Penny's neck. "You did an excellent job of using science to help athletes and to promote a healthy lifestyle."

As I watched Penny blush, I realized with a shock that what I felt wasn't jealousy. At least not entirely. I also felt proud. What Ms. Slate had just said was true. The energy bars Penny had come up with *did* solve a real problem by helping athletes to eat healthier. They'd made every bee in her dance recital buzz just a little bit better, and every peacock prance just a little more proudly. I could also tell from her graphs that she'd collected a ton of data. Not to mention that nobody could seem to stop eating her treats!

"And finally," Ms. Slate went on, "the moment you've all been waiting for. For the gold medal we have a project that looked into the science behind some ancient customs and brought them to life for us right here in our very own gym. Mummy Mayhem, by Aaron Smith." Everyone cheered, and Aaron ran up onto the stage to accept his medal. He was carrying his mummy baby doll, with the yarn brains trailing out its nose behind him. He accepted his medal, then strung it around the doll's neck, and everyone laughed and clapped louder than ever.

Finally the applause died down and we walked off the stage. The second we were out of the spotlight, I hugged my best friend.

"I can't believe that just happened," Penny said, hugging me back. "It's so unfair. You and Dominic should have won!"

I stepped back and looked at Penny, who was always on my side and never stopped cheering for me. I knew she deserved the same. I noticed Dominic out of the corner of my eye. Without our third-place-winning Rube Goldberg machine, I never would have gotten to know him better. He was standing talking to Grandpa, who looked happier than I'd seen him in ages.

Even my sister, Sarah, was grinning at me from across the gym. The talk we'd had in the kitchen the other day had made us closer than we'd been in ages.

I touched my bronze medal and held it up so it caught the light. Sure, it wasn't gold or even silver . . . but it meant a lot all the same.

"It's totally fair," I said to Penny, hugging her one more time. "Your project was amazing. You deserve the silver. And

Aaron's mummy brains thing was . . . definitely interesting," I said, wrinkling my nose a little. From where we were standing we could see him chasing Brianne and Anya around the gym with one of the bits of brain yarn on a crochet hook. "Plus," I went on, "third place feels pretty good too."

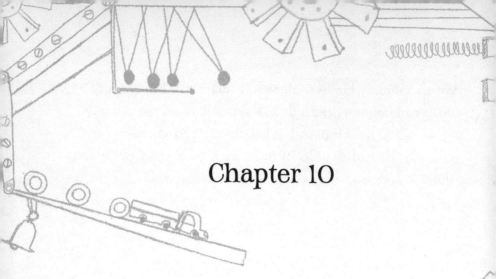

Chapter 10

B ut even though I ended up being happy enough with my bronze medal in the science fair, don't think for a second that I wasn't determined to take first place in the backyard croquet tournament at Grandpa's.

Since Dominic had started to hang out with us sometimes after school, and Mr. Petrecelli said he'd play too if we "kept the nonsense to a minimum," we'd decided to scrap our scores and start fresh. The next Friday was the first day of the new semifinals, and I did triceps flexes the whole walk to Grandpa's to warm up my swinging arm.

"What are you doing?" Penny laughed, catching me striking a strong-man pose in the reflective surface of a car window.

"Nothing much," I lied.

"She's getting ready to kick our butts at croquet," Dominic said, doing the "kick bottom" signs we'd taught him. I didn't deny it, but I didn't confirm it either. Keeping your opponents guessing is part of the game.

"Don't worry, Dominic," I said as we crossed the street and started up Grandpa's steps. "I'll show you a few of my signature moves if you want. That way at least you'll stand a chance." Then, because I didn't want him to think I was being *too nice* to him, I stuck out my tongue. He stuck his right back. Then he chased me up the porch steps. Penny just rolled her eyes at us.

Dominic and I may have been a team when it came to the science fair, but ever since then we'd been locked in some pretty fierce (but friendly) competition. Sometimes it meant we were vying for top grades in math. But other times we were dreaming up stupid contests—like who could fit the most bites of apple into their mouth without swallowing, or stand on one foot the longest. (I always won that one.)

There weren't any newspapers piled up on Grandpa's porch that day, I noticed as I let us in . . . and the lawn was freshly mowed. If anything, the place had never looked better. Since Grandpa and Mr. Petrecelli had started going out for walks, Grandpa's mood and energy had improved a lot. And, like me and Dominic, he and Mr. Petrecelli had also become kind of competitive—or maybe it was just that they were *inspiring* each other.

Grandpa had put in a new hydrangea shrub in his front yard. . . . Then Mr. Petrecelli went out and got two weigela bushes. Grandpa painted his mailbox yellow to cheer up his front porch. . . . Then Mr. Petrecelli got new outdoor lighting and a shiny set of house numbers that were so big you could see them from all the way down the street. Most recently they'd been having a debate about how to protect the plants now that winter was only a few weeks away. Mr. Petrecelli wanted to wrap them up in burlap sacks, while Grandpa said to let them be.

"He was a fussy old grump years ago when your grandma and his wife were friends," Grandpa confided in me one day, "and now he's an even fussier older grump. But he does have a way with the garden," he admitted. "And I have to say, it's been nice to have company on my morning walks, and someone to have a coffee with in the afternoons."

I could see that Mr. Petrecelli had been out that day to the hardware store to get the burlap for the bushes. It was sitting on his porch. I pushed open Grandpa's front door, expecting to hear them bickering about it, but everything was quiet . . . not to mention dark.

"Grandpa?" I called. I turned to Penny and Dominic and shrugged. "Maybe he went out to get groceries or something."

We put our backpacks in the corner. Then I flicked on the light. Something sticky came off on my hand—a big piece of Scotch tape.

"SURPRISE!"

Mom, Dad, Sarah, Grandpa, and Mr. Petrecelli jumped out from behind the sofa.

I shook my hand to get the piece of tape off and noticed that it had been holding up a string. When I tugged on it, the string released a net attached to the ceiling. The net came free, and a shower of colorful balloons rained down around a big banner strung across the room. It read: congratulations, young scientists!

"What the heck!" I exclaimed.

Penny was clinging tightly to my arm like she was about to faint from the shock, and Dominic's eyes were blinking even faster than usual underneath his hair.

"I'll get the sparkling cider," Sarah called, walking around the couch to the kitchen.

"Who wants cake?" Mom asked.

"HA! If you could have seen the looks on your faces!" Mr. Petrecelli said, sinking into Grandpa's favorite chair and pulling up the footrest.

Grandpa sat us down as the guests of honor on the sofa and handed us each an envelope. We opened them on the count of three, and inside we each found a subscription to *Science Kids* magazine.

"Thanks, everyone," Penny said.

"Yeah, thanks," Dominic agreed. "This is great. Oh, wait," he said. He went across the room and opened his backpack. He took out a small cardboard box. "I have something for you,

too." He opened it, then handed Grandpa the Thunderbolt model plane he'd taken home the first day he'd come over. "I got it working."

"Well, I'll be . . . ," Grandpa said in wonder. He took the controller Dominic held out to him and set the plane on the table. Everyone cheered when it lifted off.

And after that the party *really* got started. Grandpa turned on an old Beatles album, and we took turns flying the Thunderbolt. Mr. Petrecelli told Grandpa about his favorite places in Italy, and then—like I'd predicted—they started arguing about the shrubs in the front yard. Mom and Dad did some kind of swing dance in the middle of the room, and Penny and Sarah swapped dance recital stories.

"Well," Grandpa said, coming to sit down beside me with his second piece of cake. "What did you think of our little Rube Goldberg machine?" He motioned toward the balloons, which were still all over the floor. "Your dad and I put it together. We call it the Party-Matic 2000. I know it's simple compared to what you'd dream up." He smiled. "But we're no bronze medal winners."

"I love it, Grandpa," I said, picking up a red balloon and throwing it into the air. And I meant it. It was true that the balloon drop hadn't been complicated, but that didn't matter. The best part was that my dad and Grandpa had taken the time to put it together for us. Plus, to tell the truth I was feeling kind of done with complicated Rube Goldberg machines. Lately I'd been more into geology. Did you know that if a supervolcano were to erupt, it could rain hellfire across thousands of miles and cause worldwide climate changes? Crazy, right? Maybe next year I actually *will* do my science fair project on Mount Saint Helens. It's pretty fascinating stuff.

"Look at that," Grandpa said now, glancing down at my empty paper plate. "You need a second piece of cake."

He went off to get me a big piece with lots of icing, and while he was gone, I picked up another balloon and bapped it at Penny, who bopped it to Dominic, who tried to thwack it back, except he aimed too high and hit the banner, which came loose from the ceiling and fell down on my head.

"Dominic," I groaned, unsticking the tape that had caught in my hair.

"Sorry," he yelped, except he didn't have to apologize. If anything, I should have thanked him, because the way the banner fell suddenly gave me a *great* idea for improving Grandpa and Dad's Party-Matic.

What if, instead of just hanging the banner with tape, we strung it up on the old clothesline from the Tomato-Matic? We could also add a small weight to the net full of balloons. When you turned on the light, the string would get pulled, releasing the net—just like before. Except now when the net opened, the weight would also fall. If we attached a string to the weight, it could trigger a simple motor. The motor would start up, and the banner would unfurl across the room. Then, for a dramatic finish, we could rig up a few bags of confetti, which would explode like fireworks when they were pierced by a pin on the end of the unfurling banner. It would be so cool!

Grandpa sat down beside me and handed me my piece of cake. "You looked a million miles away there for a second, Ruby," he observed. "What were you thinking about?"

Mom laughed as Dad dipped her so low that her head almost touched the floor. Mr. Petrecelli bit his lip as he maneuvered the model plane around a hanging plant, and Penny looked across the room at me and smiled.

"Nothing much," I said, taking a bite of cake and letting the icing dissolve on my tongue. Maybe the Party-Matic was working fine just the way it was . . . even without exploding bags of confetti. After all, when you had as many good people in your life as I did, you could afford to keep it kind of simple.

31901059744609